Grown-up Education
(Anal Sex)

Amy requests that Eric show her some things. He learns.

Scarlett Collins

"I bet he wants your butt, as well. Men consistently think ladies need that, and they won't ever do."

I watched different women in the gathering laugh or look down. That was Jennifer talking, and she was prodding Jackie about her boyfriend, whom Jackie depicted as "pretty gutsy in bed."

"What do you think, Eric?" Amy's eyes tested mine as I snapped over to her.

"I believe I'm savvy enough to avoid this discussion," I answered, two or three chuckles from the women.

"Well, that is the pleasant, protected, exhausting answer," Amy scolded. "You will not mention to us your opinion?"

"Alright, I'll take the snare. Like anything sexual, I think it relies upon the lady. Some could never do it, some set up with it for their accomplices, and some truly enjoy it."

"Furthermore, I guess you have the enchantment contact to cause them to enjoy it?" Jennifer's mockery trickled out.

"I said nothing regarding me. Hell, you can find out about this if you need it. They've overviewed a ton of ladies about this, similar to all the other things."

"So what might be said about you?" Amy once more, her eyes shining.

"When did this become a conversation of my sexual coexistence?"

"You have a gathering of ladies here, discussing sex with you, and you're withdrawing? Hi? Is there any red blood in there?"

"Indeed!" I proclaimed—Amy had got me. "I realize they can enjoy it from individual experience. I don't kiss and tell, so I'm not going to uncover who; however, I realize that at any rate, one lady can have incredibly ground-breaking, soul-slamming climaxes that way."

"Furthermore, you're so secure with that? Also, that she needed it?" Jennifer once more.

"At the point when she places a container of lube in your lap and snares her finger at you while she sashays to the room, I believe it's protected to say she needs it. Concerning the climax part, it's more the compulsory side that I got on. Quakes fit. She wasn't in charge of herself."

"What's more, you didn't wed her forever?" Amy gave me a dramatic look of skepticism.
"Funny," I said. "Sex should be the lone part of a relationship. We were incredible in the sack. However, there were different issues. It didn't work out over the long haul."

"A person concedes that there's something else entirely to a relationship than sex?" Jackie joked. "I didn't realize that occurred." different women snickered while I feigned exacerbation.

6

I investigated at Amy. "So I've spilled a piece, Lady. I'm not going to keep up a single direction discussion."

"All good," she said, snickering. "I'll simply say that I haven't done it, yet I attempt to keep a receptive outlook on things sexual."

"Hold up. Perhaps we have another brave soul in the sack!" Karen noticed. Amy just stuck her tongue out.

"Discussing connections, you and Lisa have been part for a while at this point, right?" Jennifer asked me, changing the subject. "Why you're not snared with some new darling?"

"I attempt to maintain a strategic distance from the bounce back thing. That generally prompts lament. Why do you need to connect? Most likely enough time has passed for me." I needed to get a thorn in at Jennifer.

"In your fantasies, stud," she said, feigning exacerbation while different women chuckled.

They proceeded to a conversation of sweethearts and possibilities, with a lot of snickers and heckles. I participated in the good times.

After another half hour or thereabouts, Jackie peered down. "Resemble's it's the ideal opportunity for me to go. Had the opportunity to prepare for around evening time."

"I'll wager, with your brave sweetheart," Jennifer remarked. "Please, young ladies. We should allow Amy and Eric to tidy up. Incidentally, Eric, that is extremely decent of you to assist Amy with this little evening party."

"I'm trusting you spread this story around with the women. I can begin with a decent standing and coast for some time in my standard apathetic, selfish way."

That got a couple of more giggles and prods as everybody got their things and bid farewell. The majority of different people had left an hour or so back. Amy had worked effectively welcoming a co-ed combination, and the gathering had worked out in a good way. She was correct—an evening party got much more people to come since they could also make evening arrangements.

"Prepared to assist with the dishes? Incidentally, thanks such a great amount for co-facilitating," Amy said.

"Whenever, Amy. We should do it." Amy had been an old buddy of my better half Lisa, and we proceeded with the fellowship with one another after Lisa left. We both felt the misfortune when Lisa moved away; however, the open position had been ideal for her. Lisa and I both realized that we needed more going for her to remain or for me to move with her. Lisa had disclosed to me that I should follow Amy. However, it felt somewhat bizarre to hit upon a companion of my ex. Amy and I lived in a similar condominium building, so we saw each other a great deal.

"Soul-slamming climaxes, huh?"

I saw how near one another we were at the sink. The dishes turned somewhat harder to hold. "Good gracious. Not my sexual coexistence once more," I answered, grabbing for a remark.

"Hello, possibly I'm attempting to help," she said. "I have a companion who's referenced that she needed to attempt butt-centric sex sometime in the future. Would it be a good idea for me to snare you two up?"

I shook my head. "I realize it sounds insane that I'm not seizing the opportunity to get some young lady's can, yet you need to see how I work. I possibly have a good time in the sack if the young lady is making some extraordinary memories herself."

"Who says she will not have a good time?"

"It's not as straightforward as pushing inside and having her faint with joy. That might be what pornography motion pictures show, yet it doesn't work that route, in actuality. While she may suffer it and come to enjoy it in the long run, odds are it will simply be a dreadful encounter. As far as I might be concerned, butt-centric sex comes after a great deal of trust and history have developed. The two accomplices should be alright with numerous different types of sex together, and the woman must have figured out how to unwind and get delighted from that piece of her body. At long last, she's sharing an exceptionally close-to-home, private piece of herself, so she needs to confide in her accomplice. If each one of those fixings meets up, it very well may be astonishing, and she has a decent possibility of cherishing it. Then again, it's simply not something to verify in a connect."

"Sounds like an extremely adult viewpoint, Eric. Or, on the other hand, would you say you are simply searching for a bundle bargain—you know—ensured sex for some time?"

I chuckled. "I think you got me there. I'm a bundle bargain sort of fellow. Presently, if she's keen on that sort of thing, perhaps we should talk. I'm not against it, and you, by and large, have incredible companions. I'm not a major condom fellow, so ensure you get some information about getting tried, so she can rest her brain about that part of things. It's tied in with unwinding and having a good time."

"Sounds right. I'll investigate it," Amy said. "You'll be a fortunate man on the off chance that she says yes."
"Most likely. Presently, if you continue talking this way, I must get a cover on."

Amy snickered her profound, rich giggle. She delighted in prodding and messing around with individuals. "Alright, I'll let you free for some time. We should get the seats and everything off the deck."

We did that, talking about different things. Amy didn't indicate that we had been examining close subjects only a couple of minutes prior. She moved effortlessly through her home, her light hair washing between her shoulders. Ordinarily, I had seen her blend of tight body and bends, taking all things together with the correct spots. With Lisa in the image,

I had been more discreet; however, now I was delighted to have a companion so natural on the eyes. I fell quiet while I enjoyed her.

"What are you thinking?" Busted. Amy consistently appeared to get on my opinion, and she cherished calling me out. For somebody who had to stand as an extraordinary companion and all-around decent individual, Amy caused me to remain alert.

"I figure it may fall into the class of an excessive amount of data. What are you thinking?" I said, attempting to reverse the situation.

Amy gave me a long look with her penetrating blue eyes. "I think it falls into a similar classification," she said. "We should overlay up these decorative liners."

We got the last one collapsed. I put it on top of the others. Neither of us had said a thing.

"Eric."

My eyes snapped back to her. She remained there, delightful. "Indeed?"

"I didn't give you the full story previously, with my companion. Indeed, we have talked about her advantage in secondary passage sex. However, I wasn't requesting her when I conversed with you."
Unexpectedly, an unsteady inclination flowed through me. "Uh, you weren't?" I asked weakly.

She grinned, gazing directly at me. "No, Eric. Your story sounded very great, and I was truly looking for myself. In case you're intrigued, told me."

Time halted. I'm certain I looked staggered. At that point, my cerebrum got back in stuff. My heart was pounding.

"I'd love to!" I exclaimed. I was all the while attempting to fathom what was happening, yet some piece of me knew to reply with energy. "That is to say, at whatever point you would need to."

Amy chuckled. "I'll take that for an indeed, senseless kid. So how could we begin?"

"With an embrace and a kiss," I murmured, moving near her. I took her in my arms. "Goodness, Amy, you've left me dumbfounded."

"You don't need to say anything," she murmured, getting my lips with hers.

When our lips associated, something clicked inside, and I understood the amount Amy had pulled in me from the start. I needed to be more than companions, significantly more. I could feel similar waves falling off of her. Our kiss warmed up. At last, we isolated, both somewhat winded.

"Amy, you kiss incredibly."

"Much obliged to you. I figured you were a decent smoocher, as well, and I was correct," she said. "I think we'll work out together. Presently, I like your thought regarding testing, regardless of whether it eases back us down for some time. On the off chance that we hustle today, we may in any case have time."

"Lead on, Lady," I said. "Do you know a spot?"

"I think I've seen one. However, I will check on the web. Simply a sec." Amy pulled out her telephone, concentrating. Following a moment or somewhere in the vicinity, she settled on a decision.

"We have an hour before shutting. We should go—I'll drive."

My psyche was as yet in a spin while we drove down there. A ton had occurred since I woke up today.

"Eric, much obliged for doing this," Amy nonchalantly commented as she drove.
"Amy, I don't think you need to express gratitude toward me."

"Any person is fortunate just to be with me, huh?"

"Something to that effect."

Amy chuckled. "Things being what they are, you may be keen on supper? Some portion of that 'becoming acquainted with one another' thing you were discussing?"

"I'd love to, Amy."

"Great. How about we plan on it. Possibly we can stroll down along the waterway and afterward search for something."

"Smart thought. We can stroll up a craving."

We found the facility and stopped. As Amy strolled in, I saw a portion of the inconspicuous looks she was getting. The two people looked at her, and I saw the esteem in their appearances. She had a young lady nearby look of shirt, skirt, and shoes. However, they fit her bends perfectly. They took a gander at me, as well, and I got their weak grins as they understood what we were doing together at the center.

We completed and rolled over to the stream. I am accepting her hand as we began strolling. She crushed back, a grin all over.

"Happy the testing part is finished," Amy said a couple of moments later. "Be that as it may, Eric, I enjoy it. You're an incredible person. It will be a taxing week."

"In case we're imaginative, we could chip away at drawing a little nearer without getting excessively close."

"What are you thinking?" she asked, going to me.

"How about we perceive how the night works out," I answered, "and afterward, we'll examine it."

"A little secret for me to consider?"

"Precisely."

Amy gave me another of her looks, shaking her head and grinning to herself. We strolled on, simply partaking in being together. I was strolling on a cloud.

"Recall when we'd bicycle with Lisa?" Amy said as she saw a few bicycles pass by.

"Better believe it, I miss that. You intrigued?"

"I'm. I attempt to remain fit as a fiddle, and it's enjoyable to do things together. I run with my companions. However, I enjoy trekking, climbing, and different things, as well."

"How about we plan on it," I said.
"What about tomorrow?"

"Amazng."

Amy pressed my hand once more. "So what sort of food do you like?"

"As you referenced in another specific situation, I attempt to remain receptive." That got a grunt from Amy.

"Like to behave recklessly, huh?" she tested.

15

an't resist."

Amy chuckled once more. "I surmise I can't fault you. I like to play myself."

"Presently, to address your inquiry, I like anything arranged well. So on the off chance that you have a top pick, how about we do it."

"I'm the equivalent. For what reason don't we walk around, check the menus, and see what gets our attention?"

"Awesome. I'm having a great time."

"Me, as well, Eric." Amy crushed my hand once more.

We found a fish place tucked around a corner with a decent open-air territory. I had been previously and truly preferred it. We licked back with a jug of Chardonnay, discussing a wide range of things. I had consistently loved conversing with Amy. She consolidated her mind and humor with an energetic, curious mentality.

"Pardon me, Eric. I'd prefer to clean up before the food comes."

"Obviously." I got up and held her seat.

"Such a nobleman. Much obliged to you."

Amy left her telephone and handbag on the table, so I didn't go with her. I took the risk to look at her can while she walked away from the table. It was all that I recollected—adjusted and tight. She unexpectedly turned her head, found me looking, and grinned to herself before vanishing around the bend.

It was my chance to grin, thinking how Amy kept a fiendish side painstakingly enveloped by her new, young lady nearby outside.

I got tidied up myself, and afterward, we enjoyed an incredible feast of fish, wine, some plate of mixed greens, and hard bread. We both arranged to some degree light, not having any desire to back ourselves off.

"Fabulous supper, Amy. A debt of gratitude is for inquiring."

"My pleasure," she answered. "Will we head back?"

"I believe that is an extraordinary thought," I replied as my rooster began to expand.

We strolled inseparably back to Amy's vehicle and afterward drove back to our structure, proceeding to discuss a wide range of things. As we were drawing near, Amy went to me.

"I don't know precisely what you have at the top of the priority list, Eric, yet on the off chance that it includes us being together, maybe you'd prefer to get your toothbrush and go through the evening?"

"Extraordinary thought. I'd that way," I answered. I never enjoyed having intercourse and afterward resting alone. Instantly of understanding, it unexpectedly hit me that Amy knew a great deal about me. Lisa had preferred how I went through the evening, and I'm certain she referenced it to Amy. I thought about what else she had referenced. I investigated at Amy as she appeared to consider the street. It seemed like she understood my opinion.

Amy stopped and accepting my hand as we strolled to my place together. Amy had a little grin all over as she put a spotlight on me once more. She had figured out how to welcome herself in without any planning from me.

"Pleasant attempt, yet I have my place respectable. Couldn't say whether anybody would stop by subsequently."

Amy looked into it, all blameless. I snickered and received only the barest trace of a grin consequently. She followed me into my place, claiming to remain nearby as she had the opportunity to look at my drawers and cupboards. I snatched a bunch of morning garments and a couple of toiletries. When I went to the end table to get a jug of back rub oil, she momentarily caused a stir. However, she never let out the slightest peep.

"I think I have everything," I said as I moved to the entryway.

Amy grasped my hand once more. "Sure?"

"I have you, and that is the primary concern," I answered.

"You express such the prettiest things," she said as she fluttered her eyelashes. "We should go."

We strolled over to her place, and she let us in. Locking the entryway behind her, she reclined against it as though to say I have you all to myself now.

"Why not put your things in the other room," she coordinated. "At that point, we can discuss what you have as a top priority."

"Made you wonder?"

"Room's around the bend, or don't you recollect?"

I snickered and proceeded onward. I heard Amy's sink running, so I accepted the open the door to brush my teeth too. At the point when I left, she got me in her arms. In the brief moment, before we embraced close, I thought I got somewhat more definition in her nipples.

"Indeed—pondering," she said just, gazing toward me.

"Alright. Indeed, we can kiss and hold one another. That felt great previously. However, the way that we can't contact each other in specific spots doesn't mean we can't have a climax eventually, does it?"

I watched her take that in. Her eyes got wide. "You are a devilish young man, aren't you?" she murmured.

"Certainly. You'll need to concede that we will know each other significantly better a short time later."

"I'll say. I haven't played with myself for a lot of individuals."

I can't help thinking about the number of—Amy's unquestionably my sort, I pondered internally. "After we kiss for some time, I was figuring we could move to your bed, and I would give you a back rub. At the point when the times correct, you can contact yourself."

"While you will watch everything."

"Indeed. It will be absolutely hot," I answered.

"You think?" Amy shot back. "I get this. You're encouraging me to share my insider facts. Pretty sharp."

I gestured. "Anything to help a companion."

"Right," Amy droned. "Much obliged for being so thoughtful."

"You are so welcome," I replied. "I may not keep going long when you give back."

"So I will watch, as well?"

"Amy, we will do everything together. Some portion of building trust is that you will become more acquainted with my body also."

"Every last bit of it?"

"Every last bit of it."

"I can live with that. Indeed, I like it a ton. Alright, I'll oblige your little arrangement." Her eyes streaked. "You're a fortunate person, Eric. Simply recollect that."

I pulled her nearby. "I will not fail to remember." I got her lips once more.

We stood close and shared the endowment of kissing. At the point when we slowly inhaled, she grasped my hand and drove me to the couch, kicking her shoes off and pulling me down alongside her. Her hands meandered along my legs and chest, so I moved mine somewhat further. I prodded her for quite a while before I at last squeezed a bosom. She was almost driving her chest into my hands.

"Ohhhhhhhh. At last. You are a bother," she murmured.

I laughed against her lips as I tenderly played with her chest. I enjoyed what I felt under her shirt—I speculated a decent, full B-cup. Precisely what might fit the remainder of her athletic form? Her nipples stuck out and brushed against my hands as her breath got hot.

"We should attempt that rub," she said, somewhat anxious.

"Great," I replied.

Amy got up and grasped my hand once more. She drove me into the other room, gotten the back rub oil, and afterward drove me into her room. She went aside from the bed, and I caused her to divert it down from the opposite side.

"A towel to lie on might help," I proposed.

"Smart thought." Amy vanished into her washroom and came out with a shower towel. We organized it on the bed, and afterward, she moved as far as possible.

"Come here," she murmured, crooking a finger at me. We joined for another seething kiss, our hands meandering here and there one another's backs. As she warmed up once more, Amy moved her fingers to my front and began unfastening my shirt. She slid it off me and afterward raised her arms, welcoming me to pull her top off. I slid it tenderly over her head and afterward paused to rest.

"Amazing, you are lovely," I murmured. Her bosoms stood firm, delegated with hard nipples simply asking to be sucked.

Amy grinned. "Simply hang tight for when I can truly get you to myself. You are so lost, young man."

I grinned back. "I can hardly wait."

"Presently, would you say you are simply going to remain there with your tongue hanging out, or would you say you will get my skirt off as well?"

"As you wish, madam." I discovered her zipper and painstakingly worked it down, sliding her skirt down her legs and off. Remaining back up, I took in her figure, wearing just a sheer pair of pink undies.

"Your turn," she said, fixing my belt and sliding the zipper cautiously around my stressing chicken. "Somewhat energized, huh?"

"You could say that," I answered to a delicate laugh from Amy. She got my shorts off, stood, and found me and down. She gradually shut the distance between us.

"You look as great as I envisioned," she murmured, sliding into my arms. "Furthermore, I've been envisioning this for quite a while."
I moaned as she squeezed her nipples into my chest. We formed our bodies together as we kissed; my rose fighters squeezed profoundly into her intersection.

Amy hesitantly pulled back, sucking my lip before isolating. "I could do that the entire evening; however, how about we get on the bed."

I drove her over to the bed, holding her hand as she orchestrated herself on the towel. She wound somewhat and pulled my hand to the fix of her underwear. I slid my fingers under the material and gradually worked them down, helped by Amy shaking side to side. I got them off her feet and afterward pushed ahead once more.

"You are staggering, Amy," I said, and she was. Her hips erupted out into a bent, tight ass that asked to be played with. Amy glanced great in a swimsuit, and it was not difficult to perceive any reason why.

I felt her hand discover my leg and travel up, gently pulling on the midriff band of my fighters. She was a talented bother, and I got the message, sliding to the side to deliver my extending erection. Dropping my fighters over the side, I hungover to the end table and got the back rub oil. I began with a light covering on my hands. Recalling knead meetings of my own, I daintily contacted between her shoulder bones to focus her and afterward slid my full hands onto her back.

The touch was electric, with what felt like flashes flying between our skins. Amy murmured profoundly as I gently worked around her shoulders. I gradually expanded the pressing factor, feeling her muscles unwind under my fingers.

"You have wizardry hands," she mumbled, settling completely into the bed.

"Enjoy," I replied. My hands worked gradually down, going over Amy's lower back. I massaged further into her muscles, gradually loosening up them.

"Ummmm, that feels better," Amy murmured.

I proceeded, at that point moved my hands to her calves each in turn—not breaking the association. I took one hand and added some more oil. Her firm muscles undulated under my touch, while a persistent stream of moans revealed to me that she was cherishing this. I held my hands back from meandering excessively high, be that as it may, to assemble the strain.

My position staggered when I thought I saw a slight pounding movement in Amy's hips. I wasn't certain since I was manipulating her legs. However, her movements turned out to be clearer with time. At that point, the aroma of her excitement hit me. It wouldn't be well before Amy needed to reach down. My hands proceeded on her calves—I planned to make her make the following stride.

Amy attracted a long breath and afterward murmured profoundly. Her correct hand pulled away from her head and gradually meandered down. When it contacted her abdomen, she curved somewhat, and I caused her to draw a leg forward to give her room. As her hand came to under, my hands slid up onto her can.
"Ohhhhhh, God," she murmured. Her rear end pushed up into my hands.

I kept the pressing factor light, drawing out the strain. Baffled, Amy angled her back, pushing her butt upwards. I peered down and was compensated with seeing her swollen pussy materializing, her ravenous fingers sliding between her lips and sparkling with excitement. My rooster solidified to practically difficult levels—this was screwing volcanic.

Since she had admitted her need, I permitted my fingers to manipulate profoundly into the muscles of her can. Amy kept on driving into my hands. She needed to know the show she was giving me. However, it was clear she didn't mind any longer. Her fingers worked all the more immediately between her pussy lips, and a nonstop stream of murmurs and groans gave from her throat.

I slid back a piece on a hunch and lifted a knee to give her legs more opportunity. Promptly, she drew her legs separated, and I moved between them.

"Uhhhh, fuck," she murmured while her butt climbed significantly further into my hands. Amy never cussed—she must be truly turned on. I ground profound into her butt, pressing and manipulating the firm substance while the pucker of her rear-end materialized. Looking lower, I saw the dark red of her internal lips slide around her fingers and the handle of her clitoris pounding between her fingertips.

This young lady is completely lost; I contemplated internally, the sensual energy flowing through me. I prodded around her rear-end yet never went further, even as she kicked and contorted underneath me, attempting to draw my fingers internally.

Her fingers squeezed further and more profound into herself, and I examined her example, learning the mysteries of her pleasure. My eye got a development, and I admired see her other hand drop to her chest. She curved marginally and held onto her nipples, pulling her whole bosom with it. I could not accept how long and hard the nipples reached out as she moved it viciously between her fingertips. I almost blew at sight.

"Uh...uh....uh," Amy snorted with each push. The muscles of her rear end developed increasingly more tense under my hands. Her back is curved and curved.

"I'm going to cum!" she heaved. She climbed her hips off the bed, inflexible with exertion. Her butt and pussy confronted directly at me, hungry for the climax. Her fingers dove profound into her inward lips, playing her clit angrily.

"Goodness, ah, gracious, AHHHHHH!" she howled as she went over the edge. Her butt beat with the compressions and my chicken pulsated with her. Her fingers squeezed profound, gradually moving around her clit to drain all the delight it could give her. Amy surely realized how to make her body react, and I savored everything about it.

My hands kept on stroking her can as she moaned and whimpered her way back to earth. She brought down her hips. However, she kept up the sluggish back rub of her clit and nipples.

"That...was extraordinary," Amy at last said. "Much obliged to you."

"The pleasure is all mine," I answered. "It was extreme for me, as well."

"Enjoy the view?" she said, her body softly shaking with giggling.

"Better believe it, you could say that. My chicken's going to detonate."

"Helpless infant. Would it be advisable for me to help make the torment disappear?"

"I thought you'd never inquire."

Amy extended languorously underneath me. At that point, she raised, a grin playing about her lips as she looked at my extending rooster. Kissing me, she pointed at the bed. "Down," she mouthed.

I chuckled and loosened up underneath her, pulling a leg forward to give my stressing erection some room.

"Pleasant view," Amy commented as she spread oil on her hands.

She contacted between my shoulder bones to focus me; at that point, she followed her fingertips down one or the other side of my back. I moaned automatically as the fire moved from her fingers into my skin. She has wizardry hands; I pondered internally.

With leniency for my seething rooster, Amy avoided the back rub and followed her fingers down to my legs, pressing my muscles between her fingers. The shared unwinding and excitement saturated my skin. She ran near my can yet hung tight for me to take the main action.

I made it. Testing my sanity forward somewhat more, I felt Amy moved in the middle of them to give me room. I came down and shut my fingers around my rooster. I heard Amy's breath get, and a shudder hustled down my spine to know this turned her on.

Roused, I came back to Amy and measured my hand. A progression of oil into my palm disclosed to me that she got the message. I came to advance again and spread the oil around my rooster, savoring the perfection and warmth. Simultaneously, her hands went up to my can, manipulating and following over my skin. A shivering sensation spread through my appendages as I understood how profoundly Amy was associated with me.

I began pushing once more into Amy's hands, and I felt her position herself further back between my legs. She needed the view—I just knew it. So I climbed up my hips and offered it to her. Her hands crushed further, revealing to me she enjoyed it.

The pressure shocked up an indent as I shared so profoundly with Amy. My hand easily siphoned my chicken—climax was hurrying to take me. I held off as long as I could, helping the strain walk the blade edge of joy. Amy's fingers proceeded with their exceptional association.
At long last, I could keep the flood down no more, and I crushed down. Cum flooded up from my balls in explosions of fire as I yelled out my delivery. I shot many more than one rope into the towel beneath me and braved it.

-

At long last, I returned to earth. I pulled a side of the towel over the wreck underneath me and maneuvered myself down to rest. Amy's hands left my butt; at that point, I moved to one or the other side of me. I felt her weight move, and afterward, a wet pussy contacted the rear of my leg. The pressing factor expanded as she settled straddling it.

"Ohhhhhh, no doubt," she relaxed.

My cockerel mixed. Was this young lady going to bump my leg?

I found my solution as she began granulating her hips. She held her chest area off me, putting all the pressing factors between her legs. She wriggled to and fro, her juices drenching my skin. Her breathing changed to snorts as she worked herself hard. I just lay there, overwhelmed by Amy's crude sexuality.

"This is so acceptable," she heaved, pounding quicker.

"You are unimaginably hot, Amy. Put it all on the line," I answered back.

"Uh, huh."

Shortly, Amy went into overdrive, squashing her mishandled pussy on my leg. I felt the quakes start through her body as she whimpered and groaned above me. At that point, she shouted out her delivery and rode me through a long-distance race climax, her pussy flooding my leg with her embodiment. At the point when her jerks died down, she maneuvered herself down onto my back and murmured happily.

"Goodness, God, that was acceptable," she relaxed.

I laughed. "It sure felt like it down here."

I felt her snicker. "I required that after watching you. I had some genuine repressed cravings."

"Keep them going. How could I get so fortunate to meet a tigress like you?"

"This tigress has been chasing her prey for some time, and it draws out the creature in her."

"We will be incredible together; you realize that, Amy?"

In answer, I got a long kiss on my back.

When we chilled, we moved the towel far removed, and Amy went to spoon together. I put my arm around her, and she murmured and cuddled back against me.

"Much obliged to you for an extraordinary day, Eric. I loved your little arrangement."

"It's been the greatest day ever. Amy, you truly shocked me."

She laughed. "I think I amazed myself."

I floated off, reasoning that everything was direct with the world. I arose to discover her eyes investigating mine.

"Morning, sleepyhead," she said.

"Morning, lovely," I said as I inclined forward to kiss her.

Her face lit up as I pulled back. "Still content with the tigress recollections from the previous evening?" she inquired.
"It is safe to say that you are joking? On the off chance that I'd knew, I would have hauled you into my bed quite a while past."

"I suppose you loved it," she said delicately. "I needed to ensure that I wasn't excessively forward."

I investigated her eyes. "Amy, in case you're stressed that I'll feel undermined or something, set out to settle it. That was the most sizzling thing I've at any point experienced. I've generally longed for a lady who's ablaze, and the previous evening, that fantasy became a reality."

"Much obliged to you," she relaxed. "Much obliged to you for the opportunity to give up." Then she kissed me, and we both clutched it. It warmed up, the two of us sucking each other's lips. My cockerel solidified into her leg.

"Gracious, God, I can hardly wait until I can get every one of you," she groaned.

I replied by sliding my hands around until I squeezed a bosom. At that point, Amy murmured let out an unsteady breath as my fingers shut over her solidifying nipples. She kissed me wildly, similar to she was unable to get enough. We interweaved together, warming up to bubbling.

"On the off chance that I turn over, do you want to discover a spot to rub that beautiful rooster of yours?" Amy talked onto my lips.

" I want to do that," I inhaled back.

"Great." Amy pulled away and afterward moved face down on the bed. I watched her hand slide under her hips, and afterward, she turned her flushed face to me.

"I need to feel your skin on mine," she murmured.

I raised and took a gander at the sight beneath me. Amy's butt undulated to the tune of her fingers looking for her folds. I slid my chicken between her firm cheeks and settled down over her.

"Gracious, no doubt," I said. "You feel awesome."

"You have no clue," she replied. Her hips moved into an attractive granulate that sent shudders down my chicken. We pushed together, and—a veteran now—I watched Amy start her excursion to another climax.

Following a couple of moments, her breath got worn out, and her hips dove into her holding-up fingers. Her butt crushed and drained my cockerel, and my energy ran directly behind hers.

At the point when she came, I felt the shivers race through her body. Energized by hers, my climax dashed toward me. I covered my chicken profound between her cheeks and jerked over her, shooting into her back. At the point when the post-quake tremors died down, I delicately moseyed down and kissed along her neck.

"Ummmm, what an approach to awaken," Amy said. "Need to get a shower and afterward have a little breakfast before I released you?"

"Sounds awesome," I replied.

Amy got the water warm, moved under the shower, and allured me inside. "I'll attempt to stay under control," she said.

"No doubt, I would prefer not to need to give you a punishing," I replied.

"Haven't had enough of my rear end yet?" she prodded.

"Haven't begun," I replied.

Amy giggled. "You know, I sort of outfoxed myself yesterday. I needed to prod and get you worked up about my companion, yet then I understood that I had done too great a task. I truly needed you for myself, so I needed to move quickly."

"I'm happy you did. It's difficult to accept that we were simply 'old buddies' a couple of hours back. Astounding how a couple of words make a huge difference."

Amy gazed toward me. "They do, don't they?" She lifted to kiss me delicately, at that point, drove me away. "We should get this shower over before I assault you once more."

I giggled and snatched the cleanser to begin her back. She kept up a surge of energetic remarks as I went to chip away at her, blending praises like "You have the wizardry hands" with warnings like "Cautious where those fingers are going."

I got her completed, and afterward, she went to chip away at me. With seriously playing and sprinkling, we at long last completed.

"At the point when you get your hands on this body, you gotta pay," Amy said in the kitchen. "You will clean this natural product for breakfast while I get a few eggs moving."

We kept up an exuberant discussion while we ate. Amy and I had been companions for some time, and we both truly enjoyed each other's conversation. We completed, and I encouraged her tidy up.

"Weren't we doing this equivalent thing yesterday?" I said as I worked with her in the kitchen.

"Possibly, it appeared to be identical, yet it sure didn't feel the equivalent," Amy replied.

" I didn't realize I planned to get that sweet ass of yours," I droned, leaping far removed for Amy's snapping towel.

"Exceptionally amusing," she said. "Be that as it may, you will pay for it."

"Goodness, I'm certain I will; however, it will be soon justified, despite any trouble," I prodded.

"Indeed, your first installment is Friday," she said, all efficient. "You're expected here at 5 pm, and you should be prepared to put out the entire evening. Simply appear, and I'll deal with the rest."

"Indeed, Ma'am," I answered, my cockerel mixing once more.

"Alright, I surmise I can release you for the present."

"Don't we have an activity date sometime in the afternoon?" I asked, recalling our walk the day preceding.

Amy got a major grin. "We do, isn't that right? Much obliged for recollecting. What might you want to do?"

"What about bicycling? We could leave from here around 2 if that works for you."

"Awesome."

I connected my arms to her. She floated into my hug. "Amy, that was an incredible night," I murmured into her ear.

"Much obliged to you for imparting it to me," she murmured back. She came up and kissed me once more. "Presently go before I hop you once more."

I chuckled. "My standing would endure if individuals realized I was leaving a young lady who needed to hop my bones."

"Particularly if they realized it was me," she added.

"See you at 2. Bye." I hesitantly left her entryway.

I completed a couple of things and met Amy for the ride. She glanced great in her outfit and kept up a decent speed. We completed, and I dropped her off at her entryway and got comfortable for the night.

"Hi?" she explained my call that night.

"What's that thing about what amount of time it requires for a kid to call after the primary date? I needed to tell you that I'm intrigued."

"Pleasant," she replied. "You keep this up, and you may simply luck out."

"That is the arrangement," I replied. "Presently, what about a decent, virtuous date on Tuesday or Wednesday? Could I take you to supper?"

"That would be exquisite," she answered. "How about we do Wednesday."

I considered several additional occasions paving the way to Wednesday. We talked and snickered like we generally did, and I anticipated seeing her once more. At long last, Wednesday night showed up.

"So you said this was a 'virtuous' date, huh?" Amy asked as we were leaving.

"No doubt. I'm asking why I did."

"I like it—simply having the opportunity to invest some energy with you." Amy pressed my hand. "Additionally, it constructs the pressure for Friday. I can hardly wait to get my hands on you."

"I'm beginning to stress."

"Goodness, I'll get you through—never dread! I have a ton of stunts at my disposal."

"So I simply need to lie there?" I deadpanned.

"No, senseless kid. You simply need to take cues from me."

"Goodness, I get it. If I do as you say, we'll both be more joyful."

Amy feigned exacerbation. "Well, obviously, senseless. I figured you'd realize that at this point."

"I'm a genuine lethargic student on that kind of thing."

"That is the thing that I feared. I'll simply need to continue to deal with you, presently will not I?"

"You do that." We both giggled.

We shared an incredible feast of food and discussion. Amy shimmered all through—it resembled she could feel my fascination, which gave her the certainty to be significantly more herself.

"I made some great memories around evening time," she said as we returned to her entryway.

"I did as well. You're loads of amusing to be near, Amy."

"Indeed, even external the room?"

"And still. Albeit the room doesn't do any harm," I added.
"That is the place where I'm at my best, that is without a doubt," Amy snickered. She inclined in and kissed me abruptly, at that point, opened her entryway, and ventured inside. "Friday," she murmured and shut

the entryway behind her. I grinned to myself—Amy preferred her secret, and I needed to concede that she was attracting me.

The week was delayed, yet Friday, at last, showed up. The center called with the outcomes, and I understood that Amy and I planned to get significantly more cozy in the weeks ahead.

I got a few blossoms and thumped on her entryway expeditiously at five. It promptly opened, and I took in Amy, remaining in a robe.

"How beautiful," she shouted, taking them and breathing in profoundly. "We should get these in a jar, will we?"

I followed her in after she bolted the entryway. She found a jar and organized the blossoms inside it, setting it on the table. "This will look extraordinary for supper around evening time," she said. "Much obliged to you. It's exceptionally insightful."

At that point, she went to me, her demeanor hungry. The robe sneaked off her shoulders and pooled on the floor.

"You've done your best, Eric. This," she said, spreading her arms to offer her bare body, "is all yours. Also, you," she added, moving nearer, "are generally mine."

I took her in my arms for a profound kiss. My hands meandered the smooth skin of her back. Her breath blew hot in my mouth.

"Try not to prod me this evening," she murmured. "I've been standing by the entire week. Take me."

In answer, I squashed her to my chest. She whimpered in my mouth, and afterward, she groaned when my hands pressed her butt, working the firm substance. At that point, I spun her around and pulled her back to me, squeezing her bosoms while my lips looked for hers once more.

"Ohhhh, yes," she supported.

My fingers discovered her nipples, effectively erect and needing. I pulled and rolled the hard focuses, feeling Amy curve her chest into my hands. Her can drove into my hips, looking for my hard cockerel.

"I need your skin close to mine," Amy relaxed. She pulled away and went after my shirt, pulling it over my head. She stooped to pull my shoes and socks off, at that point, fixed my belt, and dropped my jeans. My fighters stuck with the power of my erection, and Amy facilitated the belt over my length. I murmured as I sprang free, and my fighters joined the remainder of my garments.

Amy brought my rooster into her hands and gave the head a profound kiss. "Coming fascination," she mumbled before ascending to kiss me once more. "Presently, were right? Goodness, yes." She pivoted and pulled my hands over her firm bosoms, arranging her butt to settle my rooster in the break.

"This feels so right, to hold you like this," I murmured in her ear.

"You have a place here—holding me," she relaxed.

I worked her bosoms over, contorting her nipples harder as she warmed up and groaned in my ear. Her butt moved around my rooster, pounding wonderful joy into the base. I let a hand meander down, hearing her consent in her relaxing.

"Goodness, God," she whimpered when my hand found the delicate hill over her pussy.

"How about we get to the bed," I directed.
"Ummmm, well," she answered, grasping my hand and driving me back. I discovered her bed turned down, with a few candles copying. I kissed her and guided her back onto the bed; at that point, she opened her legs and settled in the middle of them. Her pussy opened to my look, hot with excitement. I brought down my lips and kissed around it, at that point focused in, noticing Amy's desire not to prod.

"Goodness!" she shouted when I connected. I began lower, yet Amy pushed her hips down, driving her hooded clit under my tongue. Trying to understand, I zeroed in on the hood, hearing Amy whip and groan around me. As I felt her clit arise, I pulled the hood back and lashed the little pearl too and fro.

"Indeed!" Amy hollered. "Try not to stop!"

Amy angled her back, and I admired see her bosoms fix and hurl into the air. I leveled my tongue and let her slam against it as she drove herself to climax.

Amy got my shoulders and moaned as the fits surpassed her. Her pussy beat against my tongue, and I let her brave a long climax. At last, she loosed into the bed and tossed her arm over her eyes.

"Goodness. My. God. That was unfathomable."

"Happy you enjoyed it."

"Enjoyed it? I adored it," she answered. "Furthermore, there's something different I'll adore. Rests. I need you inside me."

I loosened up on the bed and admired see Amy position herself over me, biting her lip in focus. She set my chicken at her passageway and investigated my eyes as she gradually sank. I heaved as I felt the tight, fluid warmth of her passage. She grinned at my response, proceeding with her drop until she reached as far down as possible with a look of fulfillment.
"You feel astounding," I advised her.

"You have no clue," she reacted, inclining down to kiss me. Our tongues interlaced, telling each other our appreciation. At that point, Amy raised, setting her hands on my chest and beginning a sluggish shaking movement. I let my hands travel up her arms and move to her chest.

Amy murmured her endorsement as I squeezed her bosoms, feeling their firm weight while she inclined toward my hands.

I gazed upward at Amy, seeing trust, joy, and something more profound emanate back at me. I wanted to react, not knowing precisely what I conveyed; however, seeing it was something to be thankful for from the little grin that played at the edges of her mouth.

Amy shook somewhat quicker, and afterward, I felt one of her hands slide down between us to play at her clit. My chicken was shocked to realize that—by and by—Amy was unafraid to get what she needed in bed. I winked at her, and she grinned more extensively.

I attempted to fix this second in my mind and value all that was going on. I had a delightful lady on the back of my hips who was glad to be there. Her pussy slid around my rooster, driving a surge of red hot joy that streamed all through my body. I could see the joy course through her body too, and I could feel the pressure in her nipples as they moved under my fingers.

I loose however much I could to permit Amy to get up to speed with me. Be that as it may, her grin turned underhanded as she got a move on my chicken, curving her back to pound profoundly into me. I felt the indications of a single direction outing to climax, so I surrendered to the sensations. Amy's look changed to fulfillment as she saw that I was lost.

My skin shivered, my muscles strained, and I clasped down to draw out the ascension. At long last, the pressing factor was excessively, and I crunched up, crushing my eyes tight as my cockerel pulsated in sweet misery. Amy hammered down, adding significantly more strain to the base of my pole.

"Gracious, God," I groaned, and afterward, I snorted with each impact of cum into Amy's grasping pussy. I failed to remember everything as I discharged her.

After a drawn-out period, I opened my eyes. Amy's eyes decidedly moved back at me—she was enormously satisfied with herself. She was additionally truly turned on, and I felt her hips fire up again, and her fingers occupied themselves on her clit. I moved her nipples between my fingers, and she panted in delight.

"Yessss," she inhaled as I expanded the pressing factor. I tried to understand, pulling and contorting the hard stubs to Amy's movements above me. This time, I had the chance to watch her move to climax. Amy's eyes lost center, and her fingers sped to a haze on her clit. A become flushed spread down her chest, and her muscles strained. She dug in, held her breath, and afterward detonated.

"Ahhhhhh!" she howled, and she jolted and trembled through an incredible climax. Her face reshaped in fixation as she attempted to manage the powers spinning inside her. I watched—intrigued. This young lady reacts to sex like nobody I've at any point known.

Amy gradually recaptured control of herself.

"Golly," she said when she opened her eyes. "That was great."

"I figure you could tell how great it was for me," I commented back to her.

She grinned. "I sort of got on that. Happy I could do that to you."

"That is no joke." I pulled her down, and we communicated our gratitude to one another with our lips and tongues. I adored inclination Amy so close, and it was difficult to give up. We kissed, and grinned, and chuckled, and kissed some more.

"Prepared, Eric?" Amy, at last, said, peering down at me.

"I can't remain here until the end of time?"

Amy ignored me and gradually lifted herself off me. I jerked as my delicate chicken pulled liberated from her pussy; at that point, she extended her legs, and we imploded together.

"I believed that we could clean up and afterward recover our solidarity with supper and some discussion. I'm not exactly through with you yet," Amy said to me.

"Sounds awesome—all of it," I answered. "This date is going extraordinary up until now."

"No doubt, getting laid first is ideal for you men. I'm astonished you're remaining for its remainder."

"Indeed, you said I'm getting laid once more, so I figure I can act intrigued by whatever you're discussing for some time in any event."

"You better work hard acting intrigued, buster."

"Watch me." We both giggled.

Amy drove me to the washroom, and we giggled and prodded our way through a shower. We got some garments on and proceeded onward to the kitchen.

"Something smells incredible," I said.

"I suppose you didn't see previously."

"Not with a beautiful, stripped lady before me. No, I can't say I did."

"Happy I can stand out enough to be noticed, at any rate now and again," she droned. "Presently, would you see to the wine?"

Amy and I went through an enthusiastic night around her table, snickering and examining all ways of things. I had consistently enjoyed her conversation. However, something added a flavor tonight. We were more than companions, presently. Eventually, we got up to tidy up the table and set things aside. We moved to her love seat to complete the wine.

"What?" Amy asked when she saw me taking a gander at her. Our discussion had stopped.

"I'm making some incredible memories, Amy. You're loads of amusing to be near."

"I wager you say that to all the young ladies."

"All things considered, I do. Yet, this time I would not joke about this."

Amy smiled, at that point, glanced back at me. "It is safe to say that you think I'm's opinion?"

"I believe that we're excessively far from your bed."

"Precisely," she said, getting up and grasping my hand. "Come here," she said, pulling me back into the room. "For what reason don't we prepare for bed? I incline that we'll be nodding off after we destroy each other this time."

"Good thought."

I prepared and afterward held up alongside her bed, maneuvering her into my arms. We stayed standing, allowing our hands to meander as we got each other energized.

Amy pulled back briefly and gazed toward me. "Might you want to attempt somewhat 69 and afterward perhaps wrap up by driving into me from behind?"

"Uh, I'd love to," I croaked, my rooster driving into her leg.

Amy laughed and pulled me down to the bed. She winked at me as she put a pad under my head, licking her lips. I watched her athletic body wrap across mine, and afterward, I murmured when I felt her delicate lips circle the tip of my chicken. I kicked occupied and off kissing around her pussy, previously tasting the musk of her excitement.

Amy's ability in giving head coordinated all the other things about her in the room. I could tell that she enjoyed it, and she got on each prompt that my body gave her. While keeping the joy streaming, she did something amazing, prodding and building the strain. I did likewise back to her, not releasing anything for a long time.

"You're an evil man," she said, pulling back. "I'll require you inside me to get any alleviation."

"That is the arrangement," I said, laughing.

Amy jumped up and stooped down on the bed. "Come and get it."

I hopped up and arranged myself behind her. We both moaned when my chicken discovered her passage, and we pushed profoundly into one another.

We pulled back and pushed once more.

"Harder!" Amy instructed, glancing back at me. I put my hands on her hips and beginning maneuvering her into me, getting a snort of endorsement. Her hand wound back between her legs, and she dropped her head down again to zero in on the sensations flooding through her body.

Having depleted me a couple of hours sooner, I had the option to try not to blow it as I peered down at the inconceivable lady pushing once more into me. Amy extended before me, her tight back crookedly prompting erupting hips and an ideal ass. I felt its firm forms with each stroke and the contact undulated outward from my crotch, adding to the delight transmitting from my rooster.

"Gracious, no doubt!" Amy energized as we found a cadence and bobbed against one another.

"Amy, you feel inconceivable!" I replied, at that point lost myself in the vast delight of Amy's pussy.

Amy whipped her hair over her back, and I saw that her face was flushed with excitement. Her fingertips stimulated my balls as she worked her clit hard. Amy groaned with each push, and her enthusiasm pulled mine alongside it.

From profound inside, I felt the sparkle of climax flare into a fire. Simultaneously, I felt Amy's avaricious fingers speed into a free for. Her groans expanded in pitch.

"I'm close, Eric. Harder!" Amy smashed into me, and I hammered back accordingly, resolved to give this young lady what she needed.

A few crashes later, Amy delved her fingers profounded into herself and held them, simply beating once more into me.

"I'm coming!" she moaned and writhed around my chicken. I watched the ligaments of her shoulders stick out while a profound flush surrounded her neck. My enthusiasm took off to watch her cry and whip through her climax.

Abruptly, I was heaved over the edge, hanging in space, while a cold radiance shot out through my appendages.

"Ahhhh!" I howled as my climax surged up to guarantee me. I fell into sweet alleviation, shooting my delivery into Amy's grasping pussy while my body jerked behind her. She pushed back hard into me and held there, amping up the joy moving from my cockerel.

We remained combined for quite a while, at times shaking through a spike in the phosphorescence. I let my hands float over Amy's legs, back, and ass, feeling the smooth skin as she murmured underneath me.

At last, she talked. "Goodness. That was fabulous."

"It was the equivalent for me, Amy. You're stunning."

"Much obliged to you, Eric. I truly required that."

"I was glad to help. Tell me whenever."

"Continuously prepared to take care of a young lady?"

I chuckled. "You have me there."

"Great. I have a ton of requirements. You'll be occupied. Presently, you prepared for me to relinquish you?"

"Not actually, however it should happen at some point."

"Helpless child. Here goes."

I whimpered as my cockerel slipped free, hearing a laugh consequently. We both loosened up on our backs, moaning in unwinding. I moved to my side and hungover Amy.

"That was an incredible night, Amy. I'm happy I remained for everything."

"So the supper and discussion were a little cost to pay for the extraordinary sex?"

"No, they were an exorbitant cost. However, the sex was justified, despite any trouble."

Amy feigned exacerbation. "Whatever, darling kid."

I inclined in to kiss her, pulling back an evolving tone. "Truly, I would check myself fortunate just to eat with you, Amy."

Her eyes mollified. "Much enjoyed, Eric." She kissed me once more, moderate and delicate. "I'll dream well around evening time."

"Me, as well. Goodbye."

Amy turned, and I spooned behind her, floating off with considerations of how fortunate I truly was.

Morning came, and I got up to find Amy's shining eyes investigating mine.

"Morning, darling kid. I trust you didn't think you were accomplished for the evening."

"With horny, destitute ladies, I'm rarely done," I replied, attracting her for a kiss.

I chose to zero in on her pleasure toward the beginning of today, warming her up and afterward reprimanding her pussy until she shouted out in climax. At that point, Amy pulled me up on top of her, and she bolted her lower legs over me as we tenderly shook together, our tongues profoundly twined. I came powerfully, groaning into Amy's mouth. We kissed our way back to earth.

"What an approach to awaken," I advertised.

"Very great, Eric. My commendations. You have a sorcery tongue."

"Proves to be useful here and there."

"Keeping penniless women fulfilled?"
"Precisely."

"All things considered, it worked. Incidentally, I'm dazzled." Amy's hand-wound around to my butt. "You went through a whole night with me and never went for my can. Much the same as you said in your little discourse regarding the matter."

"You had any uncertainty?" I giggled. "Furthermore, I realize I will arrive in any case. What's the hurry?"

"Pretty sure about yourself, right?"

"That is the reason I endeavored to have a sorcery tongue," I answered. "Had the opportunity to keep you fulfilled so I can get what I need."

"Furthermore, what, ask to tell, is that?"

"One moment. I don't spill every one of my mysteries so without any problem."

"Ooooh, I do love a test," Amy whipped back. "We'll perceive how long you last."

I just winked in answer.

Amy and I got tidied up and made breakfast together. We cleared out, with plans to get together again for supper. After an extraordinary supper, we were strolling up from the vehicle. Amy put her hand in mine.

"Might you want to go through the night once more?"

"Love to," I answered.

"I think you'll enjoy what I have arranged," she said, winking. I figured I would. I was beginning to value Amy's room way. She needed to lead, here and there, she needed to be driven, and regularly she would react to whatever waves were coming from me.

Amy let me into her place and accompanied me to her visitor restroom. "You'll discover a toothbrush and a couple of different things there," she said.

"A little arrangement ahead of time?" I prodded.

"Never harms," she said softly. "Gracious, and dress for tonight is exceptionally easygoing. I'll meet you alongside the bed?"

"Sounds awesome," I answered.

I prepared, draped my garments in her visitor storeroom, and moved to her room. I thought about what she had as a primary concern. My cockerel figured it was something acceptable because it extended out, good to go.

I sucked in my breath as Amy's body materialized. Her eyes seethed up at me through brought down foreheads. Her nipples extended out on her firm bosoms. Her legs nimbly brought her over to me.

"Happy to see you're energized for me," she said, gently circling my cockerel in her grasp.

"How should I not be?" I answered, attracting her for a kiss.

We kissed long and hard, our breath warming up. Amy pulled me down on the bed and tossed me a pad, snickering as she rode me. I utilized the pad to prop up my head to arrive at Amy's pussy, effectively wet with want. I felt her lips kiss my cockerel as I took the main pass with my tongue. After a piece, I let my hands meander and touch her rear end.

"Uh, huh!" Amy empowered. She came to under my legs and did likewise, as though to say I'll do it maybe.

I grew somewhat more striking, ultimately measuring my fingers over her valley, however not inside. Amy's murmurs empowered me, and she wound under my hand, attempting to get my fingers further. Amy had lifted my knees to improve access, and her fingers kept on imitating mine.

At last, I let a finger momentarily haul across her rosebud. Amy shocked in fervor, groaning around my rooster and pushing her can into my hands. She was certainly OK with this. After a second, I felt her finger contact me in a similar spot. I meandered some more, at that point, let another finger drag, getting another groan. This continued for some time, with Amy getting increasingly more animated. She flew off my rooster to inhale and afterward utilized a hand to hang on. I gave her leniency and slid my fingers straightforwardly over her rear end, touching the harsher skin.

"Yessss," Amy murmured. I lapped at the dampness moving from her pussy, as I felt her fingertips hold up at my indirect access. Amy moved, and her clit crushed into my tongue. Her breath blew teased my chicken while her body strained and shuddered.

"Goodness, God, don't stop!" Amy shouted. I took her to the highest point, and she bounced off with a cry of delivery. Her body shook all over me in a beast climax. I felt her rear end beat to the constrictions hustling through her pussy; everyone joined by a moan of alleviation. I celebrated in Amy's all-encompassing ride and kept my fingers possessively on her rear end while she returned to earth.

"What occurred?" she said in a precarious voice. "I came truly hard."

"How about we talk later. I need to be inside you now."

"Smart thought," Amy snickered. She flipped around and sank onto my post. "This what you need?"
"Definitely," I groaned back.

Amy began pounding her hips once again me, a grin all over. "Come for me, infant."

I did precisely that, giving her ride me access to an incredible climax. Amy had prepared me with her response to my fingers on her rear end, and I came long and hard, allowing Amy to watch me squirm and groan under her. At the point when I returned, I investigated her eyes.

"Turned on a piece, were you?" she asked, her eyes moving.

"You could say that. I just had this hottie come hard everywhere all over."

Amy reddened. "I'm nearly humiliated by how much that turned me on."

"Indeed, we're drawing nearer to 'soul smashing an area."

Amy chuckled, her body setting little stuns along with my cockerel. "I couldn't say whether I can deal with it anymore. Goodness."

"I believe there's a smidgen of the no-no and releasing yourself. Yet, a great deal of it is only that it feels great."

Amy squatted down to kiss me. "Great. A debt of gratitude is for that."

"Any time."

Amy feigned exacerbation. "Duh. You'll gladly get your hands on my butt any time?"

"Precisely. You have one evaluation A, top-notch ass."

"Whatever else, grade-A?" Here eyes streaked a test.
"Everything, Amy. Everything."

"That is the correct answer, Eric," she said delicately. She inclined down to kiss me once more.

We got up to clean up and snuggle together for the evening. The following morning, we chuckled our way through a shower, had a fast breakfast together, and afterward, I returned to my place to prepare for work.

Tuesday night, we were eating together.

"In this way, we're both welcome to the large party Saturday," Amy noticed.

"Furthermore, you're considering how we ought to present ourselves?"

"Something to that effect," she said, her easygoing words at chances with the bursting force of her eyes.

"Maybe we ought to present ourselves as beau and sweetheart," I proposed. "It would give a cover to us being together to such an extent. Individuals will begin to see our bundle bargain."

"That may bode well, Eric. Figure you can fill the role?"

"It will be an appearance for me, Amy. Don't worry about it."

"You express such the prettiest things," she answered, coming around to sit in my lap. She remained there some time, and afterward, we shared her bed.

Saturday showed up, and I drove Amy over to the gathering. I am accepting her hand as I encouraged her out of the entryway.
"Such the respectable man," Amy said, plainly satisfied that I was openly showing friendship. I didn't deliver her hand as we stepped to the entryway, and I kept a firm hold as we strolled into the home. You could nearly feel the responses and recalculations as everybody took in our new relationship, transmitted more powerfully than any assertion. Amy emphatically radiated, making some incredible memories with a particularly striking animal adjacent to me.

Jennifer gave us a long look, positioning an eye at every one of us. "Alrighty then. I can't say I'm amazed. Eric's wild ways interesting to you, Amy?"

"He's a finished fallen angel in the kitchen!" Amy spouted dramatically. "I'm adapting to such an extent!"

"I...see," Jennifer deadpanned. "All things considered, make certain to tell me the high focuses."

I even snickered at that one. Jennifer winked, and afterward, her face got agreeable.

"I believe it's extraordinary. I like you both, so I'm cheerful. You even figure out how to go through with your companions, so it's all acceptable."

We got comparative ribbing from every other person. Individuals were glad for us and made statements like "finally" or "happy that is no joke." We remained together for some time and afterward circled independently as the night extended. Sooner or later, I advanced back to Amy.

"Searching for a decent time, infant?"

"Definitely. Would you be able to help me discover one?" she shot back to snicker from her circle.
"I understand that armies of failing to meet expectations folks have made you tainted, yet I can fix you from that," I replied.
"Oooooh. I like the test in that," she said, sliding an arm around my abdomen. "I'm sooo tainted," she added, feigning exacerbation to her companions. There were a lot of snickers.

"I'll simply stand by until I needn't bother with words any longer," I said, to more snickers from the gathering.

"Women," Amy said, murmuring. "I have another person to assess. I better kick him off. Goodbye."

We left to a melody of heckles. "Back off of him!" "Evaluation hard." "You've given so many F's. Cut him some breathing room!" I halted and pulled Amy close on out the entryway, nailing her with a profound kiss before everybody. She put her hands around my neck and nailed me back. We left in a burst of applauding and cheers.

"So you unquestionably weren't humiliated to concede being my beau," Amy saw as we strolled to the vehicle.

"Chicks burrow the public warmth thing. Little cost to get under their skirts," I replied, gazing directly ahead.

Amy grunted. "Riiiight. Yet, it's working."

I investigated and winked. Amy crushed my hand.

We got to her place, and Amy pulled me inside.

"You're doing quite a few things, Eric," she said, shaping her body to mine.

"I need this sweetheart/sweetheart thing to work," I replied, kissing her.

Amy almost assaulted me by then, getting me rock hard with the waves falling off her body. She pulled back and looked at me without flinching.

"I truly need it to work," she relaxed.

We made extreme, sentimental love that evening. Some kind of limit had been crossed, and we both felt it. Our lips never left each other after she pulled me on top of her, and I felt her climax as my own. We dozed tangled together, secure in our relationship.

"Wake up, sleepyhead," Amy said the following morning. "We're going running, and we need to get out before it gets excessively hot."

"Wouldn't we be able to simply have intercourse and tally the exercise that way?" I answered lazily.

"No motivation to settle on a decision, Eric," Amy said sensibly. "We can do both. You will long for my rear end on the run."

"That run is sounding better constantly. What are you sitting tight for?"

"Whatever, darling kid." Amy tossed a pad at me.

We got moving and taken off the entryway. Amy glanced great in her running outfit, and I tried "following" her at whatever point we expected to run a single record. I heard a laugh each time.

As we were chilling off toward the end, Amy investigated.

"Along these lines, we certainly need a shower and maybe some morning meal. Something else?"

"No doubt," I answered. "Presumably, you need to recuperate in the wake of attempting to stay aware of me. What about a loosening up back rub after breakfast?"

"Recuperate your can," Amy shot back. "Be that as it may, the back rub sounds decent. I'll take it."

"Great. Perhaps it tends to be somewhat cozier than last time."

"It should be," she answered, eyes moving. "Presently, how about we get that shower."

We tidied up, and Amy arranged an extraordinary breakfast.

"Phenomenal, Amy," I commended. "Will we clear the dishes and get the back rub moving?"

"No," Amy replied, getting up. "Give up directly to the great part."

"I like your style," I chuckled, grasping her hand.

I got Amy chosen a towel and spread the oil over her back.

"No doubt, Eric, that feels incredible," she mumbled in a casual, simple voice. "Exceptionally decent after an exercise."

"Continue to unwind, Amy."

She sank further into lethargy as I worked over her back. I kept the pressing factor firm this time, keen on extricating her muscles from the run before bringing back the strain. Amy took cues from me, remaining loose as I worked down her legs. I pressed the enthusiastic muscles between my fingers, valuing the exertion she put resources into her body.

At last, I moved to her butt, yet again kept the pressing factor firm—not having any desire to energize her excessively fast.

"Ummmm," she murmured while I felt her muscles respecting my hands. I kept this up for some time; at that point, I continuously decreased the pressing factor. She murmured at the change, gently pushing her rear end up into my hands.

As my touch helped a stroke, Amy's body warmed up, wriggling and pushing underneath me. I felt her legs isolated, and the primary whiff of hot pussy arrived at my noses. I let the pressure work until I could feel the dissatisfaction in her body. That is the point at which I at long last let a finger brush around her rear-end.

"Yessss," she murmured, climbing her rear end up to welcome me further. I reacted, prodding around the delicate spot until she was gasping under me. Yielding, I brushed over her pucker.

"Gracious, God," she groaned. I gazed upward to see her eyes firmly shut, nullifying all the other things to focus on how my hands were doing her.

My fingers invested increasingly more energy over her most private spot, until where they won't ever leave. Amy's body undulated to the sensations, joined by a constant flow of moans and murmurs.

My other hand tested under her hip, and she promptly really tried to understand, moving up barely enough for me to slide under her. She let out a guttural groan as my fingers discovered her aroused and smooth pussy.

My rooster swayed when she spread her legs and climbed her hips off the bed, adjusted on her chest and knees. I was an ass man, and Amy had her body in the most sexual position conceivable—gave up to wring the greatest conceivable joy out of my hands.

After sawing through her pussy for some time, I slid my fingers up to crush and caress her unmistakeable clit. Amy went wild, pushing and gasping her way extremely close to a dangerous climax.

At long last, her body went inflexible, shuddering in my grasp. I cinched down on her clit, and her climax detonated, undulating through her pussy and ass as she wailed into the sheets. After a since quite a while ago arrangement of post-quake tremors, I tenderly slid my hand away from her desolated clit when she chose the bed. Nonetheless, I kept my different fingers possessively on her butt, and she once in a while wriggled into them. Sooner or later, she let out a long murmur.

"Nice, Eric," she mumbled. "That was mind-boggling; it has a sense of security and warm."

"Your body reacts so well," I reacted in appreciation. "I could play with you throughout the day."

"My body could become acclimated to that!" she reacted. "At any rate, I realize that you're getting a charge out of this as well."

"You have no clue, Amy," I reacted, peering down at my hand stroking her executioner ass. "This is awesome."

Amy conversed with me a short time longer, relating how my hands had made her cum hard. She didn't appear to be humiliated about my hand staying on her butt. She proceeded to tenderly shake under my fingers, plainly appreciating the play.

"On par with this feels, I'd prefer to give back in kind," Amy, in the long run, said. "Why not rests, Eric?"

"Happily," I replied.

"Face up this time," she coordinated. "I have an arrangement."
"Oh goodness," I reacted, getting a chuckle as I loosened up adjacent to her.

"I don't think you need to stress, Eric," Amy said as she settled close to me. "Aren't my arrangements in every case great?"

"Advising me that I should just allow you to assume responsibility?"

"Isn't it in every case better that way?" Amy said, inclining down to kiss me.

"It's difficult to contend when I'm sleeping with a delightful lady," I said as she inclined away once more.

"Particularly when she's going to go down on you," she added. I moaned as her lips shut over my shaft.

Amy gave an exceptional penis massage, sucking and prodding my rooster until I was squirming under her. Her hand stroked my balls and afterward headed out between my thighs to urge me to open up. I did, and Amy slid further, rubbing my perineum.

"Yessss," I murmured to support her. Sooner or later, her hand voyaged further, running ever nearer to my indirect access.

"Ahhhhh," I moaned as Amy discovered it. She worked to and fro between my rear end and prostate, driving me into a free for.

"I'm going to cum!" I said in an unsteady voice, attempting to caution Amy. She reacted by sinking significantly further around me.

I tried to understand and just dropped into the occasion—Amy's awesome lips sliding along my shaft alongside her hands unquestionably examining along with my butt. A cold warmth prickled outward from my crotch, and I kept the conduits down to the extent that this would be possible, going inflexible with the exertion.

Amy sucked hard, building the pressing factor until it was relentless. I detonated into her mouth, moaning sounds torn from my throat as I shuddered underneath her. My climax moved on in a long, fulfilling set of impacts, depleting the repressed energy conceived from feeling Amy's body cum underneath me.

Amy rode with me the whole time. At long last, I loose once again into the bed, and she delicately dialed her lips down my cockerel and her fingers from

"You are astonishing; you realize that?"

Amy's face lit up. "Obviously, yet it's ideal for getting with you," she said as she inclined toward kiss me.

We at last isolated sometime after that, and I completed a couple of errands. Amy was certainly making it harder to stay aware of the ordinary pieces of life—we just fit together so well that the time flew.

Next Friday, Amy met me at the entryway exposed once more. I sure loved this present young lady's style. We kissed and caressed each other right inside the entryway, and she maneuvered me into her room. I saw a jug of lube on her end table, and my cockerel was shocked at the greeting. As Amy got my garments off, I turned her around and pulled her against me.

Amy moaned as my rooster slid up between her cheeks, and she shifted her head back to secure her lips on mine. My hands discovered her bosoms, the nipples hardened and needing. Amy's skin sizzled against mine.

"Damn, young lady, no doubt about it," I said as we paused to rest between kisses.

"Goodness, no doubt," Amy inhaled, crushing her butt much harder into my bar.

We twined together for quite a while, neither in a rush to break our bond. At last, Amy began gradually advancing toward the bed, pulling me alongside her. At the point when she arrived along the edge, she pulled away and masterminded herself face-down on the bed, her arms padding her head. She connected and got a handle on the lube, giving it back to me.

"I believe it's an ideal opportunity to get somewhat more private," she expressed in a guttural voice.

"One 'broadened closeness' coming up!" I said.

Amy's body shook with her chuckling. "For what reason am I enduring you once more?" she pondered out loud.

"Since it feels so great," I answered, manipulating my hands into the cheeks of her can.

"Gracious, better believe it, truth be told," she murmured. "It feels great."

At that point, Amy worked up, so I immediately circumnavigated around to her butt, getting a lot of support.

I stroked around the puckered bud until Amy was wriggling underneath me, her butt driving into the air. I went after the lube with my other hand.

"Thought you'd never arrive," Amy mumbled when she heard the snap of the cover.

"Everything in due time," I answered without any problem. "We'll take this at your speed, so center around the joy." I grasped my hand from her rear end, watching her pucker pound into the air, and afterward followed a surge of lube over my pointer.

"Ohhhh," Amy moaned as my smooth finger discovered her rear-end once more. She pushed restlessly. However, I disputed, not having any desire to surge this. I orbited around, squeezing further. Amy moved and pushed her lower arms forward, preparing herself to crash into my hand with more power.

"Feeling better?" I asked her.

"Indeed, Eric. I need more," she coordinated as her body squirmed on the bed.

"Alright, Lady," I replied. I pulled my finger away to sprinkle somewhat more lube, at that point supplanted it, and delicately pushed. Amy moaned in fulfillment. My finger slid into her pucker, and Amy wound her canto and fro, attempting to get more inside herself. I watched my finger sink past the main knuckle; at that point, I gradually hauled it back, simply allowing the tip to stay inside her.

"Nooooooooo," Amy moaned in disappointment, turning her body considerably harder.

Where did this young lady come from? I contemplated internally. I pushed my finger further this time, feeling the hot dividers of Amy's rectum. I let my finger follow them, getting a groan of endorsement. Amy sorted out my example and didn't say anything negative as I pulled back out once more.

With each stroke, my finger covered itself further into her profundities. At last, I reached as far down as possible.

"Ohhhhhhh, that feels better," Amy gasped, driving herself back to smooth my different fingers over her cheeks. As I pulled back somewhat, she shook forward; at that point, she met my next internal stroke with a solid drive into my hand.

We got into a mood, and my chicken solidified to a bar of steel to see Amy drive herself into my hand with such surrender. Her body contorted and kicked under me, and her butt gripped around my finger.

I came to under Amy with my other hand to discover her clit.
"Goodness, God, yes!" she shouted as my fingers discovered her folds. Her substance ran openly from the heater of her pussy. I outlined her unmistakable clit and began lashing it without leniency. Amy went wild, her body wringing all of the delights it could.

When Amy began snorting with each push, I admired see her face squeezed into the sleeping cushion. My finger kept on siphoning all through her butt, and I felt the strain work in her body. The snorts filled in pitch, and afterward, she pushed back hard. I slammed my finger profound into her and felt her inward muscles start to pulsate.

Amy moaned into the sleeping cushion as her can and pussy detonated in my grasp. I excited to her sphincter beating fiercely around my finger, coordinated by compressions in her pussy. There isn't anything more wonderful than a lady in the climax, and I had the chance to watch an incredible one as Amy's body jerked and shivered through incalculable fits.

When Amy began to descend, I gradually pulled out my fingers from her pussy and let her choose the bed. At that point, I tenderly backed my finger out of her can, getting a whine as her sphincter shut behind it. Amy turned her head and took a gander at me.

"Amazing," she said, "that was extreme. Possibly soul-slamming," she added modestly.

"It looked pretty damn great from here," I said. "You were delightful."

Amy becomes flushed. "Delightful, huh? I get it bodes well since you're an ass man."

"Adequately genuine. Be that as it may, I believe I'm discovering somebody who's as attached to her rear end as I am."

Amy reddened considerably more profound this time. "It's sort of humiliating the amount I loved that."

"You can generally act naturally with me," I reacted tenderly.
"Trust me, I wouldn't be this route with any other individual," she stressed.

"That is the reason I'm a fortunate person."

"No doubt," she shot back.

"Presently, would it help to adjust the score on the off chance that you did likewise to me?"

Amy grinned. "Definitely. That could."

"I'll be directed back." I got up and washed my hands in the sink, at that point, snatched a towel, and strolled once more into the room. Amy was her old self, sitting on the bed with the lube in her grasp and an eager look all over.

She guided me down and continued to work my rear end over with excellent strokes. At the point when the time had come, she copied my movements to slip her finger profoundly into my can, and afterward, I curved underneath her similarly as she had done. I ascended to give her another hand room. However, she wasn't prepared at this point. After she had tormented me enough, she, at last, lubed her other hand and slid it around my rooster, siphoning me to an unstable climax. After braving the result, I settled down on the bed, and she perfectly pulled the towel from under me. She removed consideration, facilitating her finger from my butt.

"That was quite hot, Eric. I could feel everything pulsating inside you."

"Better believe it; I believe it's a significant piece of lady's sexual training."

"I see. Furthermore, what else is significant?" she asked archly.

"Everything in its legitimate time," I said.

"What rudeness, addressing an adoration goddess like me about instruction. Nonetheless, I'll let you pull it off since you're so acceptable in bed. Be that as it may, you better keep it up."

"Trust me, Amy, I expect to."

"Great. Presently, I think I'll tidy up a piece, and afterward, we can sort out how to manage the remainder of the night."

That was quite simple—great food, discussion, and wine, and afterward, another round of incredible sex. We woke up the following morning and went for a climb, chuckling and bantering the entire time. We had consistently been acceptable at exchanging insidious insults, and we returned to Amy's place feeling energetic, chuckling at the residue and sweat on our skin.

Amy spun out of my hands when she shut the entryway and went to confront me. Her eyes moved.

"I'm feeling somewhat underhanded and devilish," she said. "Got any thoughts?"

My cockerel yanked upward as an image framed in my psyche.

"Definitely. I think you'll like it."

"Goodness, goody, I can hardly wait," she said. "Am I stripped?"

"I figure I uncovered might be a superior word."

Her face took on a more out-of-control look. "At that point, I'm beginning at this point." She reaches down to pull her shirt over her head. I stripped alongside her, and soon we stood confronting one another.

"Go get an extra sheet and bring it into your front room," I said. Amy curved an eyebrow, at that point gestured and cushioned off. I went into her room to snatch the lube and met her close to the sliding glass ways to her overhang. I pulled the drapes aside, allowing light to fill the room. Amy gulped.

"Presently, I don't figure anybody can truly see in here. However, you never know without a doubt, isn't that right?"

She shook her head, at that point, gasped as I dropped the lube on the floor to help her spread the sheet.

"Indeed, Amy, I will play with your butt. You will be down on the ground, wriggling around my thumb covered somewhere down in your indirect access while my different fingers play with your pussy. My other hand will cinch your nipples, and I'll be watching everything, and I mean the world."

Amy pulled the sheet tight with me and afterward came over, pulverizing herself against my body.

"Gracious, God, I need that," she said.

I bolted my lips to hers, at that point, slid my hands around her back, going all over her spine. My fingers discovered her could, and she groaned her endorsement. I possessively measured the firm tissue while Amy hauled her nipples across my chest. I pushed a leg forward, and she promptly rode it, bumping with need. At the point when I felt the wetness of her excitement, I came up and pushed her shoulders down. Amy didn't should be told—she sank to her knees and afterward to her lower arms. Her rear end stuck enticingly into the air, and I touched the delicate skin, feeling the dull current stream between us. I let my eyes wander over her body, seeing the pucker of her sphincter, the swollen pink of her pussy and her clitoral hood, and afterward glancing over to see her nipples distending from firm bosoms. I wrapped up by considering her face, seeing the lost demeanor of somebody in profound excitement.

My fingers went ever nearer to her butt, and Amy moaned when I brushed my thumb across it. My other hand discovered her bosom, and I rolled the fat nipples between my fingers. Amy curved her chest down into my hand, and I expanded the pressing factor, setting off a groan of endorsement while she drove her rear end into my other hand.

My thumb presently drifted over her sphincter, scouring and pushing the somewhat unpleasant tissue while Amy kicked underneath me. I let my fingers float down over her cut, and they discovered her swollen and wet—time to move this along.

Amy opened her eyes as my fingers left her body, and a little grin played about her mouth as I sprinkled lube along with my thumb. At the point when I supplanted it on her rear end, she squirmed her hips to attempt to get me inside her. I took it extremely lethargic, feeling her external ring open to me. My thumb facilitated inside a piece and stopped at her inward ring. I moved to and fro, prodding the ring to open, while my other hand changed her nipples once more. I gazed toward her face, and my rooster was shocked at the suggestion of seeing her eyes investigate mine as I opened her can.

I investigated, seeing a combination of weakness, enthusiasm, expectation, and delight flutter across her highlights. I felt her push and her inward ring loose, allowing my thumb to slide into her. I gradually worked to and fro while Amy curved her rear end into my hand. In any case, she looked profoundly at me, looking for a window into my considerations. Her eyes enlarged in shock at something in mine, and afterward, she shut them and covered her face into the sheet, murmuring joyfully to herself.

My thumb had worked into the flare of the subsequent knuckle, and I let my different fingers spread across her rear end, giving her another sensation. She continued shaking and pushing once again into me, driving my thumb to the root. I looked as it slid in further, her rear end extending to oblige the meaty base.

"Yessss," she murmured when she felt my hand press profoundly into her can—my thumb was covered as far as possible in her gut. I followed her movements, coaxing mostly out as she shook forward and afterward driving profoundly home when she pushed back. She gave a little snort each time I reached as far down as possible, plainly lost in the sensations. I watched her experience that her back curving and turning underneath me; at that point, I got her nipples once more, crushing hard.

"Uhhhhhh," she groaned, driving her bosom into my hand. Her longing took off higher as I worked her body over, and I could feel her pressure fabricate. I watched her nipples stretch as I pulled and bent.

"Gracious God, good God, gracious God," she wailed into the sheet, wracked by her dim need with no unmistakable route for discharge. At the point when I felt she was unable to take it any longer, I moved my fingers to her shuddering cut.

"Ohhhhhhhhh, God," she breathed out, her alleviation obvious at discovering some exit from her sweet misery.

Her pussy ran openly, juices streaming down her legs. I gloried in how hot this young lady had become and slid further behind her to improve see.

My fingers rubbed the external lips, pulling away as she curved her back and pushed, attempting to get them on her clit. At long last, I yielded, sliding around the hard pearl, standing pleased from its hood. I kept the pressing factor delicate from the outset. However, Amy had different thoughts, curving her hips to pound her clit against my fingers. Her groans got more limited and higher in pitch, and I realized she was near a huge climax. I cinched down on her clit, squeezing it between my fingers, and she screamed into the sheet. A couple of more bucks of her hips and her body went inflexible.

From profound inside her, I felt the explosion start. Amy shouted as her pussy and ass grasped around my fingers, and her whole mid-region shook with its power. I even felt the waves contact her expanded bosom, her nipples beating in my fingers. Amy's body pulsated for a long spell, and she whimpered and moaned through it, her eyes firmly shut.

In the long run, her climax worked out, and her wracking cries died down. I gradually backed my thumb out of her can. However, I kept it possessively at her passage. She moaned with satisfaction.

"On the off chance that you need my can, it's yours," she said delicately. My cockerel shuddered with the consent in those words.

"Not exactly the time," I answered, "yet trust me, we'll arrive. My rooster is almost blasting after watching you experience that. You alright with me beating into you from behind? I will not keep going long."

"If it's not too much trouble, snatch my hips and take your pleasure, Eric," she reacted.

I arranged behind her and situated my iron pole at her passageway. She slugged back, spearing herself. I snorted with the vibe of her tight sheath grasping my cockerel, and I grabbed hold of her hips and drove myself into her, again and again. Amy remained directly with me, pushing back each time until she can be smoothed. Before long, I could feel the pressing factor fabricate, and I kept down as long as possible. At the point when it became too a lot, I pulled her back firmly against me, crushing her hill against the underside of my cockerel. My cum flooded past in white-hot planes, shooting somewhere down into the profundities of her pussy. I snorted with each impact, appreciating my delivery from the pressure of watching Amy's sensual showcase. When the flames subsided, I backed out and fell on the sheet, pulling Amy down with me. We kissed profoundly; at that point, she settled her head on my chest. We rapidly feel snoozing.

Awakening after a reviving rest, I felt like 1,000,000 bucks. I could feel Amy's heart thumping against me, and the world felt right.

Amy blended, and afterward, she delicately lifted her head to investigate my open eyes. Hers were clear and substance.

"That was...exactly what I required," she said. "You had me totally, yet I could feel the amount you gave it a second thought. Much obliged to you."

"Amy, the thing I like about you best is the point at which you give me a sincere much obliged for accomplishing something that I was biting the dust to do in any case. You are so welcome."

Amy grinned. "On the off chance that I'd knew what a cruel darling you were, I'd have grabbed you from Lisa and never let you go. How could I get so fortunate?"

"I ask myself that consistently."

Amy's eyes hooked on to mine and dove deep once more. She found what she needed, for I saw a grin turn up the sides of her lips.

"You truly do," she pondered. We investigated each other's eyes for some time longer. At long last, I broke her look and pulled her lips to dig for another kiss.

"Prepared to get a shower?" I inquired. "We're each sort of grimy."

Amy giggled. "No doubt. Help me up?"

We made it into the shower and exchanged washing obligations. As Amy was soaping my rear, her hands meandered until she held my balls. She brought her lips near my ear.

"So I need to ask, how could you be ready to hold back from taking my rear end when I offered it to you?"

I snickered. "I would have come in two strokes if I had done that."

Amy snickered back. "I hadn't thought about that."

"Truly, however, there's a period and spot for that. As you're most likely sorting out, a major piece of butt-centric sex needs it. At the point when you're unpleasantly baffled, and you need it so terrible that you'll effectively get it, that is the correct time. You realize it will not do any harm, and you realize it will fix what afflicts you. We'll arrive, and we'll investigate each other's eyes again as you sink and fill your rear end with my chicken. Trust me; I need this however much you do."

"I'm getting horny tuning into you. I can hardly wait," Amy said energetically. I felt her grin behind me. "It would appear that another person can hardly wait all things considered."

We wound up having intercourse in the shower, Amy squeezing me against the divider and taking me inside her. I wondered about her sensuality—weak one moment and persistent the following.

That night, we went to supper with our companion's group and hung out at Jackie's home. We returned to Amy's late and headed to sleep; I longed for Amy the entire evening. The following morning, I woke up to locate her, taking a gander at me.

"Curious what you might be thinking, sleepyhead."

"You truly need to know?"

Her eyes enlarged. "Particularly now."

I murmured. "Amy, do you know how suggestive that was yesterday? That is to say; I realize we're chipping away at butt-centric sex together. In any case, you are past volcanic. At the point when you viewed at me yesterday as I was playing with your can that was about the most sizzling thing, I've at any point seen. You tap into some dim current that is wild and untamed, yet defenseless and cozy. On the off chance that you revealed to me that you were a sorceress, I'd trust you."

Amy took a gander at me for quite a while; at that point, I grinned. "Be that as it may, Eric, I am a sorceress."

"I trust you. You have an enchantment blend of young lady nearby newness, smarts, and something underhanded. At that point, you wrap everything inside a bundle that is very simple on the eyes. I think about the thing I'm attempting to say is that I'm completely devoted to you, and I'm an exceptionally fortunate person."

Amy's eyes held mine. I let her test. At long last, she grinned again and talked delicately, her words standing out from the burst in her eyes. "In case you're attempting to get into my jeans today, that is no joke."

I burst out snickering. "I neglected to add the comical inclination."

"Isn't that what they say about an arranged meeting?"

"Better believe it. So why not screw me senseless, Miss Blind Date?"

She feigned exacerbation. "I generally succumb to the sentimental ones," she said to herself. At that point, she bounced on top of me instantly of power, sticking me to the bed and assuming responsibility. I didn't do anything aside from reacting as she warmed me up and continued to screw the heck out of me. I strongly suggest it.

We recuperated with her leftover on top of me, her tousled hair falling across my chest.

"Don't hesitate to reveal to me how fortunate you are whenever, Eric."

"Gee, I think I've found a spell over you."

"Goodness, better believe it, and I'm defenseless against it." I could feel her grin on my skin.

****

Tuesday night discovered us chatting on the telephone.
"Thursday will be an unpleasant day," she advised me. "We have an audit with a significant customer, who is requesting. We've been getting ready for two or three weeks; however, we hope to be obliterated. I'll be a worried zombie when I return home."

"I have a thought that will cause you to disregard senseless things like what your customer thinks. Intrigued?"

"Allow me to figure. It includes me exposed?"

"Shockingly, it does."

"Well, obviously, I'm intrigued!"

"At the point when you return home, call me. At that point, jump in the shower and clean your insidious pieces great. I'll give myself access with this convenient key you gave me," I taught.

"Thursday doesn't sound so terrible, all things considered."

"That is the soul! Presently, get your rest, and thump them dead."

After work Thursday, my telephone rang.

"It was fierce. However, we endured OK. Also, it truly assisted with having your little secret to anticipate. I'm jumping in the shower now."

I gave a few minutes and let myself in, going to her room and lighting a few candles that I brought. I opened up a jug of wine and two or three glasses, put a French nation stew on her oven, got the plate of mixed greens in the cooler, at that point stripped down, and folded a towel over my midriff.

Before long, I heard the water stop, and Amy arose a little later, a towel folded over her.

"Goodness my, I like," she said, as she took in the candles and the glass of wine I was giving her.

"Great. Presently plunk down close to me and enlighten me concerning your day."

Amy truly had a hard day. As she completed her glass, I took it from her; at that point, I got behind her on the bed and began rubbing her shoulders and neck as she proceeded with her story. At last, I came around and stood her up.

"Continue to talk," I taught.

I reacted to her; however, I followed kisses across her body at whatever point I wasn't talking. I began at the rear of her neck, plunging between her shoulders. I covered her arms, at that point tenderly facilitated the towel from around her, and proceeded down her back.

"It will be difficult to get done with revealing to you this story," she said after a murmur.

"That is the ticket. Continue onward."

I let my hands bother her nipples as I worked down her back. I kissed momentarily down one cheek of her rear end, at that point, began dealing with the backs of her legs. In front, my hands reflected what my lips were doing toward the rear. I could feel Amy getting diverted. The murmurs came to an ever-increasing extent, and she moved her weight between her legs. I climbed, kissing delicately across both ass cheeks.

"Ahhhh, that feels better. I think you have the essence of the story," she said.

"Is it accurate to say that you are certain? I would prefer not to miss anything."

"All things considered, you're not missing anything up until now," she said, squirming her can in my face.

"Reveal to me somewhat more. What happens the following time you meet this customer?"

I grinned to myself as I tuned in to Amy, attempting to center. My lips circumnavigated consistently nearer to her rosebud. I heard little murmurs blended in with her account, and she offered a lovely short response.

"Sounds like you're loosening up quite well, yet I need no doubt. Why not outfit here on the bed?" I encouraged her up and got her down on the ground. "Here's a pad for your head."

"Such a courteous fellow," she snickered, resting her head and curving her back.

"Presently," I proceeded, "I'm attempting to loosen up you, however knowing you, you may begin getting worked up. If it's not too much trouble, feel good to deal with any little issues you may have in such a manner."

"Try not to stress."

"Amazing." I moved back behind her. "Presently, were right? Gracious, indeed, kissing your magnificent ass."

I began once again, working gradually toward her middle. Amy's breathing got, and the aroma of her excitement contacted me.

"Ohhh, God," she groaned when I first touch her butt with my tongue. Gradually, tortuously, I contacted it all the more frequently, looking as her can began squirming noticeably all around.

At last, I gave her what she needed, lapping profoundly across her pucker. I felt her hand slide between her legs to begin playing with herself. I rotated profound strokes with lighter excursions around her edge.

Amy began driving into my face, and I smoothed my tongue to let her discover the pressing factor she needed. Her hand moved quicker and quicker, and I could hear the wet hints of her pussy getting pulverized.

I felt the natural shiver of her body straining for a major climax. She contorted her can into my tongue, totally offered over to the delight flowing through her body.

Amy's breath came in snorts and pants; at that point, she went inflexible, yelling into the cushion as the seizures undulated through her pussy and ass. My tongue was blessed to receive a fantastic view, and it got each quake.

I remained with her as her climax faded away. At that point, she whipped her head around.

"Inside me. Presently!" Amy told her fingers directing me. Her hands never left her clit as I stroked into her, and she came soon after I shot an extremely fulfilling load inside her.

We got done with returning to earth, and I sat down close to her on the bed.

"Pretty unusual, Eric," she said. "You certainly caused me to overlook my day."

"It was my pleasure. I had loads of fun. I love your can."

"I can tell. I surmise if I at any point advise you to kiss my butt, you'll help thinking about what I mean."

"No, I will not," I said.

Amy chuckled her rich giggle. "No, I suppose you will not." She went to embrace me. "I cherished it. I'm happy my rear end turns you on."

"No doubt. Presently, will we evaluate some supper?"

"I was trusting that I was smelling something lovely. I'll need to concede that I didn't see up to this point."

"Happy to hear it. Please." I drove her up, and we got dressed and cushioned into the kitchen, carrying the jug of wine with us.

Indeed, I enjoyed an extraordinary supper with Amy. As we were waiting in the course of the last glass of wine, she fixed me with her eyes.

"Eric, I need to say the amount. I enjoy how you're doing me. You're taking me to places I didn't know existed, and I'm cherishing what I'm discovering there."

"Amy, I can't reveal to you how much fun I'm having taking you to those spots."

"I can see it in your eyes. In any case, there's something else. You realize I've been an enthusiast of yours for some time. What I didn't comprehend was how much the genuine article outperforms my fantasy."

It's practically difficult to acknowledge an incredible commendation like that. I sat back, staggered. At that point, I acted with my body when the words wouldn't come. I got up and grasped Amy's hand, at that point, pulled her up for a long embrace. At the point when we isolated, I got my tongue once more into gear.

"Amy, that caused me to feel great. I'm a truly fortunate person."

"Your boots you are," she reacted. "Be that as it may, I'm a truly fortunate young lady, as well."

As you would figure, our shared reverence society got us all worked up. We had intercourse again that night, and I staggered out of Amy's bed promptly the following morning to return to my place and start my day.

We went through Friday out with companions, at that point, went to supper Saturday with a couple of something else.

"Care to go through the evening?" Amy asked as I was driving us back.

"Difficult to leave behind that offer," I replied, my dick solidifying in my jeans.

"Would you be keen on allowing me to coordinate our sporting exercises tonight?"

"I could go for that," I replied, my dick getting considerably harder. "What do you have arranged?"

"Uh, uh, intelligent kid. That would demolish the fun, wouldn't it?"

"Alright, Lady, I'll let you keep the secret."

We returned to Amy's place, and she drove me inside.

"Do you confide in me, Eric?" she asked, a grin all over that was directly out of a 2nd-grade jungle gym.

"Indeed, yet responding to an inquiry like that consistently leaves me somewhat stressed."

Amy fluttered her eyelashes. "Stressed over sweet little me?"

"Presently, I'm certainly stressed!" I replied, to a chuckle from Amy. "In any case, I'll trust you."

"Great, you will love it. Presently, could I request that you close your eyes?"

I shut them, my different faculties in a flash increasing. I stressed to hear Amy move, yet could get nothing. At last, I hear the delicate cushioning of feet from me, at that point returning behind me. I hopped when I felt the blindfold slide over my eyes. Amy tied it tenderly, at that point grasped my hand, and drove me down the lobby. We went into a room, yet it didn't feel like her room. Amy's hands came around my front to unfasten my shirt, at that point tenderly simplicity it from my shoulders. My shoes and socks were eliminated; at that point, Amy got my jeans off. It took somewhat more work for her to control the belt of my fighters over my uncontrolled erection. Her game was turning me on.

Amy grasped my hand and guided me to the bed, masterminding me on my back, with my head serenely on a cushion. I felt a stirring aside, and a delicate material was circled over my correct wrist. My chicken stressed much harder as I heard Amy stroll around the bed and circle another band over my left. I stayed still as I heard and felt her do likewise to my lower legs.

"Generally excellent, Eric. You do truly confide in me, and I can't reveal how great it causes me to feel. Why not attempt your bonds? Wouldn't have any desire to ruin the fun if they aren't working right."

I moved my arms and legs, discovering I could move two or three inches.

"Hello!" I cried as Amy's hands stimulated me. I attempted to roll away or do anything. However, it was pointless.

"Presently, I'm fulfilled," she said, yielding. "Sort of enjoyable to have you at my kindness."

"What was I saying about being concerned?"

"I like you somewhat stressed," she said, chuckling.

I detected Amy cushioning around the space to a few objections, and afterward, I felt her trip onto the bed with me and reach forward. Shockingly, I felt her draw the blindfold off. However, I was considerably more stunned to find that I was unable to see anything.
"Indeed, Eric, it's completely dark in here. I needed to perceive how our different faculties were elevated when we were unable to utilize our

eyes. Your faculties will be particularly elevated since you can't utilize your appendages. You've been driving me to some extraordinary places recently, yet I'm the sort of young lady who likes to keep the score even. My chance to take you on an excursion."

"Lead on, Amy," I said. "I'm yours."

"That is the reason I like you," she murmured as I felt her inclining down.

My lips felt the gentlest touch possible. My sensitive spots moved, stressing for additional, as she gently brushed her lips against mine. At that point, I felt her path kisses over my face and neck, an electric buzz snapping off my skin any place she contacted.

"Goodness, God," I moaned.

"You're shuddering," she murmured.

"I can't accept how you're not kidding," I murmured back.

"Trust it," she replied, and afterward, I felt her hands softly brush along my arms. Rushes dashed through my body as Amy followed over my bonds and afterward my hands. She worked her way back to my chest, and afterward, I felt her lean down once more.

"Fuck!" I jolted against my restrictions as her tongue contacted my nipples. I felt Amy laugh as she delicately, excruciatingly, did something amazing over the two of them. I didn't have the foggiest idea the amount a greater amount of this stunning torment I could take.

It was then that I felt her tongue slide down my midsection. I jerked and shivered under her considerations—every last trace of my skin snapped with expectation. My chicken was stressed as it would blast.

At last, Amy worked her way to my crotch. She delicately blew a breath at my cockerel, and I leaped to feel frigid fire dart away from my overly sensitive skin.

"Jesus, Amy!" I panted.

She disregarded me, contacting the tip of my chicken with her tongue. I kicked and squirmed at my restrictions, even though I realized it was miserable. She blew once more, and I shuddered from the chill at the tip of my chicken.

For what appeared to be an unending length of time, Amy prodded me pitilessly. She was all over the place, and she was no place. My superheated cockerel would have smoked on the off chance that it could. Licks, breaths, kisses, and contacts—Amy kept me speculating.

At that point, I felt her moving around on the bed, and I detected that she was hanging over me. A hard stub just touched my lips, and I got the clue, tenderly opening them to investigate Amy's nipples. Without my different faculties, it was a disclosure. The skin was delicate at this point, hard under, with little knocks and surface along the length of her nipples. I additionally felt the little knocks of her nipples and underneath the snugness of her bosom. I could hear Amy's delicate breath as she kept herself still for me, causing me to know her in a new manner. I wondered about how much this lady could communicate with her body.

Amy gave me quite a while to play, and afterward, I felt her nipples pull out while she moved once more, the heaviness of her thighs choosing either side of my face. My noses were overflowed with the aroma of hot pussy, and I paused while she settled down. Like her nipples, her pussy softly brushed my lips, and I delicately investigated the folds of her pussy with all the sensitive spots available to me. I felt her external lips, swollen and hot, shuddering marginally as I contacted along with them. Then, I moved to the inward lips, milder and flushed with warmth and dampness. I, at last, let my tongue investigate, feeling everything once again. Fulfilled, for the time being, I licked with more power, abandoning investigating to pleasuring. Amy's delicate murmurs revealed that I was doing it right, and I felt her prodding my rooster once more.

Inevitably, Amy pulled away and pushed her hips back. I shut my mouth and by and by felt a light touch at my lips. This time, it was her upper pussy, and I investigated how the inward lips united at a little hood. I could feel the strain in Amy's thighs as she kept herself down— almost certainly, she needed to slam her clit down all the rage. I tested around the hood and afterward felt under. Amy heaved despite herself, and I thought I felt the little pearl of her clit. However, it was difficult, no doubt. I kissed and snacked in this spot, and Amy began to squirm above me. At long last, getting my tongue included, I delicately whirled around her hood, quietly letting the strain assemble. Amy cooperated, never pounding herself against me.

Amy's pleasure constructed increasingly elevated, and I could, at last, be certain that her clit was standing glad. I whirled around it with my tongue, tenderly lashing it from all sides.

"Gracious, God," Amy groaned. My cockerel could feel her worn-out relaxing.

Her pussy was a wet heater, dribbling onto my jawline. My nose was overwhelmed with the hot tang of her excitement. Her thighs shuddered with the strain.

Detecting all was good and well, I delicately sucked her clit between my lips.

"Ahhhhh!" she heaved. I tightened my lips and let her drag the little pearl out between them. I opened them once more, and she got the cadence, driving her clit in again as I sucked.

From Amy's ambiguous snorts and wheezes, I could tell that she had lost all origination of anything besides the sensation of her clit hauling through my lips. Her pitch got higher, and I realized that she was preparing for a gigantic climax.

Out of nowhere, she went inflexible, simply holding her pussy above me. I could hear the strain in the quick cries coming from her throat. I sucked in her clit as profound as possible and hung on.

The primary fit dashed through her body, gripping every one of her muscles much harder than they, as of now, were. I heard her cry as the unwinding wave went through; at that point, the following compression came significantly more grounded. Her pussy and clit beat as expected, and my delicate lips caught everything. Endlessly it went, Amy shouting with delight so hot it was almost torment.

As the compressions diminished in force, I tenderly loosened my tension on her clit, realizing it was touchy. Amy was almost wailing above me. I automatically thrashed against my bonds, needing to hold her through the defeat.

As it was, I just tenderly rubbed around her inward lips with my lips and tongue, keeping the positive sentiments rolling while she settled through the glimmer.

At last, I felt her draw a full breath in and afterward breathe out in a long murmur.

"I don't have the foggiest idea what occurred there," she mumbled. "That was so extreme; it was startling."

I just gestured under her, and she hopped, laughing at the contact.

At that point, I hopped when she plunged her lips down over my chicken. She snickered, back in charge. Her hips immediately spun away, and I felt their weight settle down with one leg on each side of mine.

Delicate fingers situated my stressing chicken, and afterward, I felt the head enter her smooth passage. I hung tight for her to sink around me.

She didn't. She delicately shook above me, washing the top of my chicken in the fluid fire. I wriggled under her, attempting to get more inside her. Even though I could not see anything, I could feel her grin transmitting down at me. I realized she was cherishing this—my pleasure relied totally upon her.

At that point, the bitch discovered my nipples with her fingers. Delicately stroking, softly scratching, she sent shocks of flow out through my chest. Combined with the sweet desolation consuming the top of my cockerel, she made them shudder under her.

"Amy!" I croaked wretchedly.

She overlooked me. She was a cruel sorceress, playing my body like some evil spirit instrument. Unexpectedly it hit me with frigid lucidity— Amy was imparting her mystery secrets to me. Something basic and basic moved from her, a dim force that shot into my body.

I offered myself to her and let my body react in kind. Something moved from me back to her, an acknowledgment of her clouded side and the noting yell from mine.

We both heaved at the association. To open yourself to another, and afterward to discover what you've generally longed for; all things considered, that doesn't occur all the time.

Amy pummeled down, immersing my rooster in her blazing passage. One hand went to my mid-region, stimulating me to occupy me from the lovely joy transmitting from my cockerel. I knew where the other hand was going.

Amy shook her hips hard, siphoning my cockerel in fluid velvet. Her fingers played her clit, taking herself alongside me. I whipped and squirmed under her, attempting urgently to move away from her stimulating fingers and attempting frantically to remain with them. I didn't have a clue where torment finished, and joy started any longer. It didn't make any difference.

In that obscured room, my faculties centered down to two things: Amy's touch wherever on my body, and afterward an intuition of energy streaming between us. I plunged in, following that turning, beating channel back to its source in obscurity openings of Amy's being.

A feeling of glow coursed through me. At this point, it was not my chicken; however, my whole body consumed under Amy's light. I rose with it, and afterward, a white-hot wave writhed through me. I hollered out as another took me, a sensation of careless happiness filling my general existence. Through our association, I could feel something comparative flowing through Amy.

At that point, I stopped existing.

Afterward, I knew that floods of happy delight had moved through me and that Amy had shouted out with the equivalent. At that point, there were no words for what occurred or for long it went on.

I, at last, recaptured consciousness of myself, and I felt the post-quake tremors shaking through me and the full weight of Amy's hips laying on mine. At that point, I felt it—the association was still there. Not as hot or splendid as in the past, but rather as yet connecting us—seething and prepared to jump to fire once more.

Different sensations came through to me: Amy's breathing, without rushing as she recuperated. Her hands squeezed profoundly into my chest as she upheld her weight. My chicken secures inside her.

We remained together like this for an all-encompassing time. Neither of us needed to break the spell.

At long last, Amy murmured profoundly.

I chose to talk first. "Amy, I don't have the foggiest idea what occurred. However, I'll never go back again."

"We'll never go back again. It hit me, as well, and it unquestionably hit us."

"Who are you?" I pondered so anyone might hear. "Great, agreeable, and charming, yet also dim, puzzling, and cruel. How could I get so fortunate to meet you?"

"I believe you're meeting the individual you've allowed me to become," she replied. "I've never at any point considered allowing anybody to see that previously."

"I trust I will see it on a lot more occasions," I said. "I'm simply in wonderment. You are a sorceress."

"What's more, I cast my dull spell on you, Eric," she said, her voice intelligible and bursting. I felt our association jump once more.

Amy let that wait; at that point, she inclined down and squashed her lips to mine.

At last, I felt her facilitate her hips up and gradually let go of my rooster. She stopped at the head and eased back significantly more, reducing the stun of her lips cruising by. I jerked. However, I enjoyed her mindfulness.

She moved off the bed, and I felt my restrictions being delivered individually. At that point, she returned and settled next to me. I folded toward her and spooned into her back. She snatched my arm and squeezed it profound to her chest, murmuring cheerily. Without sight, my different faculties were as yet honed. I could feel her heart pulsating, moderate, and fulfilled. I feel snoozing with our association still unblemished.

We woke following a soothing evening, actually tangled together. Faint bits of light spilled through the dim covering that Amy had on the windows.

"Mmmmmmm," she murmured, nestling further into me.

I held her, believing her satisfaction stream across to me.

"I could remain here everlastingly," she said so anyone might hear.

"So could I," I replied. "Do you feel it like I do?"

"Indeed," she said, "However, I need you to mention to me what you feel."

"It resembles I have a channel of profound energy associated with you, Amy. It's delicate at this moment. However, it consumed hot and brilliant while we were having intercourse."

"That is it," she said. "I believe the association our mystery sides made with one another."

"You're correct. It resembles I know your genuine nature, Amy, and they go with mine."

"I've never set out to impart them to anybody previously," Amy said. "I'm so glad I did with you."

"From sorceress to blameless young lady," I pondered. "You are every one of those things."

"Furthermore, do you like it?"

"No, I love it," I said and gave her a long crush.

"I do as well," she inhaled and cuddled back once more.

I settled against her and let my hand meander over her legs and hips. It wasn't sexual this time—we had consumed that with extreme heat for the present. Rather we just existed and let our skin express our association.

Ultimately, my stomach thundered, and Amy laughed.

"I'm happy I didn't do that first," she said, chuckling. "I surmise we'll need to get up and grab a bite."

"How about we do it."

We gradually got up, and Amy drove me to the entryway. Before opening it, she took both of my hands.

"Recall what occurred here," she directed, her voice blasting once more.

"I swear I won't ever fail to remember," I said officially, the words sounding valid between us.

"I discharge you," she got done with, leaving me to consider what she was delivering me from. It sure wasn't the dull spell she cast over me— I could, in any case, feel that. I realized she needed me to ponder.

She pulled the entryway gradually open to allow our eyes to change. Daylight gushed through her place—we had dozed late.

She gave me a robe, taking one for herself. "Allow me to get you some morning meal," she said.

"Those were deliberately positioned," I said. "Had this arranged out?"

She looked into it, a smile all over. "Eric. What occurred—you don't arrange for that."

I giggled, profound and long. "No, I suppose you don't. In any case, some piece of you did."

"Are you so sure it was me?" she asked, her blue eyes blazing.

She spun around and was stepping to the restroom before I could reply. Her inquiry hit me like a thunderclap, tossing my psyche into disorder. What had happened the previous evening? What had she begun, and what had I begun? Could I at any point know? I understood that there was a ton behind those blue eyes of Amy's.

We prepared and had breakfast together, Amy controlling the discussion away from the prior night. We got dressed, and afterward, she showed me out. She looked profoundly at me.

"Invest some energy with your heart, Eric. I will invest some energy with mine." She kissed me and delicately pushed me out the entryway. "Call me."

I staggered back to my place and got dressed for a long bicycle ride. In no way like actual work to clear the head. I pushed out and required around thirty minutes to get into a mood, my muscles heated up, and the energy streaming.

I, at that point, sank into my heart, detecting it siphoning life through me. I opened myself to my emotions about Amy. The original was a mass of dread—the dread that I would lose myself in her and dread that I could be profoundly stung. I investigated my dread, realizing that I needed to respect it to move past it. Amy should mean a ton to me for me to be this stressed; I contemplated internally. I pushed past and investigated further.

The following inclination was dread once more—dread that I was succumbing to Amy explicitly, yet not totally. I felt further into my heart and realized this wasn't correct. I adored being around her for herself.

As I investigated further, it hit me with power. I needed to impart my heart to Amy, and I was unable to live without her. At that point, I was lost, and the lone way was to twofold down and drew nearer to her. Such a lot had happened so quick—however, it felt so right.

I investigated that for some time. Did I feel any uncertainty? Was there some concealed notice signal in my heart?

No, you moron. She's the one for you.

"Much enjoyed," I said so anyone might hear, laughing at myself. "Happy that is settled."

What's more, it was—I could feel that profoundly. I rode with that feeling for some time.

With such minor things settled as who I needed to consume my time on earth with, I could proceed onward to different subjects, similar to what the heck happened the previous evening. Unmistakably, Amy needed to even the score a bit. I had been the lead for most of our relationship, and she needed to reverse the situation and take me on an excursion. She almost let go completely when I was lashing her clit. Interesting how I was the one tied up; however, I had her completely devoted to me.

Powerless to resist me. Perhaps that is what she implied when she suggested that I had begun it the previous evening. Perhaps she was reacting when she cast her spell on me. Whatever she was doing, she did something extraordinary for herself.

Then again, as I looked through my heart, I could feel that she had been working her spell on me for quite a while—in any event since the day of our gathering together—and most likely a whole lot sooner. She had risked a great deal to uncover her inner feelings to me the previous evening. In any case, I could feel the association with her—something I had never imparted to anybody.

I quit thinking and just rode home in an ocean of sentiments and feelings—all great, yet also terrifying in their power.

That night, I called her.

"Ideal to hear your voice," Amy said. "What did you do the entire evening?"

"Precisely what you said. I took a long bicycle ride and invested some energy with my heart."

"Furthermore, did you learn anything?"

"Indeed. A lot, truth be told."

"Anything you'd want to share?" Her voice was light and well disposed of. However, I could detect her listening eagerly.

"It was quite ground-breaking stuff, Amy."

"To make sure you know, I went through the evening with some ground-breaking stuff of my own."

I realized that she needed—no, she required—for me to go first in this little game. Also, a lot was on the line. Twofold down.

"The principal thing I felt, Amy, was a mass of dread. Dread that I was losing myself and that I could be profoundly stung."

Her voice got delicate. "We need to place extraordinary trust in those we care about. It implies a great deal that you're placing that trust in me."

"I do confide in you, Amy. Also, I pushed past that dread. In any case, the following thing was another type of dread. This time, about me. Could I be certain that I wasn't simply succumbing to you explicitly? That is to say, I needed to concede, the sexual part has been wonderful."

Amy's lilting chuckle got through the telephone. "That is putting it mildly, and I enjoy the hidden supplement. What did your heart advise you?"

"Not to stress. I was succumbing to the total bundle for quite a few reasons."

"I...you...thanks." Amy's voice was thick with feeling.

"Something more that I'll discuss around evening time. I inquired as to whether there was some uncertainty, some admonition signal that I should think about."

"What's more,

"Nothing."

"Eric." I could feel the quiver in her voice. The line got genuine calm. "Eric—to make sure you know—my heart is exceptionally cheerful at this moment."

I could feel her keeping down the cries. "Amy, why not offer your heart sometime later? I think we've had a major day, and it's most likely an ideal opportunity for some rest."

"Much obliged, Eric," she murmured. "No...Thanks. Goodbye."

"Goodbye, Amy," I replied and cut the association. She required the opportunity to herself.

The following morning, I had a message on my telephone.

"Would I be able to prepare you supper?"

Simple three-letter answer.

I halted by the flower specialist and showed up at Amy's entryway for certain blossoms. She is a real sense, hauled me through the entryway, and squashed me in a hug. Her words arrived in a surge.

"Eric. You need to know. My heart feels precisely like yours. What you said—it was far beyond what anybody has at any point said to me. Do you realize how upbeat I am?"

"It just felt right."

At that, she burst into cries. My tears followed hers.

"I guaranteed myself that I wouldn't cry," she cried into my shoulder.

"Amy. You can generally act naturally with me." I embraced her tight.

We, in the long run, unraveled, bashfully giggling at one another's red-rimmed eyes. Amy drove me to a seat and served me an incredible supper, her eyes shining each time I got them. It didn't take a lot of knowledge to see that she was coasting on a cloud. I glided with her, scarcely mindful of what we discussed.

When we completed, I expressed gratitude toward her, and afterward, I rose to help her reasonable the plates.

"No," she directed. "I'm serving you around evening time. Your responsibility is to converse with me while I move this set aside."

Amy wrapped tidying up and returned to me, offering me her hand. She lifted me and kissed me, at that point maneuvered me down the lobby, and shooed me into the restroom.

"Meet me in my room in almost no time. Try not to wear excessively," she coordinated. I tidied up, taking as much time as necessary, at that point stripped. I strolled back to Amy's room to think that its lit with a few candles. Amy remained by her bed and coaxed me over.

She slid into my arms. I felt the smooth skin of her back as she kissed me. We shared the joys of one another's lips, and afterward, Amy tenderly pushed me back onto the bed. I lay back while she rode me and drove me through a night of sentimental lovemaking. My primary recollections were of her eyes, looking profoundly into mine as she delicately shook above me, and the grin that played about her face. We never looked away, even as we each jerked in the climax.

We lay together and talked; at that point, Amy began kissing me once more. In the long run, she turned and rode my face, driving us through a 69 meeting that got us both worked up. This time, she lay back and pulled me on her, and we kissed profoundly while we gradually worked to another fantastic peak.

"Much obliged to you for going through the night with me," Amy said as we recuperated. "I delighted in having the opportunity to investigate your eyes the first run-through and afterward feeling your tongue in my mouth the second."

"Any time, Amy," I answered. "I'll do it above, I'll do it beneath, I'll do it behind, and I'll do it genuine sluggish."

"What's more, you'll do it in my home, and you'd likely do it with a mouse," Amy noticed drily. "I would be advised to get these candles out before I need to tune in to substantially more good times TV."

At the point when she got back in bed, I pulled her nearby.

"Amy. Much thanks to you such a huge amount for having me over. You're unique, and it's extraordinary that your heart is falling for a comic."

"I wish I could help myself, yet I can't," Amy said as she cuddled further into my arms.

I tenderly stroked her back until she subsided into rest, and afterward, I followed her.

We gave each other a couple of evenings off after all the feeling that had poured out throughout the most recent few days. Nonetheless, I had welcomed Amy to supper with a gathering of companions Friday.

"Just on the off chance that you consent to return to my place for a nightcap," she had advertised.

"I want to do that," I said.

Jennifer, with her standard instinct, cornered us at the bar before supper.

"Both of you appear as though you're on a cloud. Things should get going truly well between you."

Amy peered down, a become flushed crawling up her cheeks. I could feel my face getting warm.

"Presently, you've disclosed to me everything," Jennifer said. "I'll be forgiving and let you be, Amy. What's more, you, Eric, I believe you're dealing with her?"

Amy and I both snickered—a piece anxiously.

"Goodness, my, both of you are lost. I could pose more inquiries. However, I think I know the appropriate responses." Jennifer's face brides out into a grin. "I can't reveal to you how cheerful I am for you both. Presently, we should guide the discussion to more secure subjects."

"Extraordinary thought," I croaked out. Jennifer winked.

We overcame supper with no more off-kilter minutes. We strolled up from the vehicle with our fingers interlaced.

"Still need that nightcap?" Amy inquired.

"Anything at your place would be extraordinary," I replied.

"Anything?"

"Sweetheart."

Amy feigned exacerbation and got me through her entryway. She bolted it behind her and went to me.

"Would I be able to be your nightcap?"

"I'd love that, Amy."

She snickered and shut the distance between us. Her delicate lips discovered mine, and we failed to remember our chat. Her body smoked in my arms, her breath hot and her lips unyielding.

At long last, Amy pulled back to take a gander at me. She took every one of my hands and attracted them behind her to lay on her butt, which wriggled against them.

"Eric. What did you say about being appallingly horny and baffled? I feel that at this point."

"You mean..?"

"Indeed, you know precisely what I mean."

"How about we go slowly," I said warily.

"Be that as it may, don't be excessively mindful," she said. "I need this."

"Need it terrible?" I prodded.

"You have no clue," she murmured. She shut the distance between our lips and kissed me savagely. My cockerel hardened to steel in my jeans as she ground into me. My hands went here and there, her back as she warmed up. I simply sporadically wandered down to her rear end, prodding her barbarously.

"I ask for from these garments," she relaxed. I encouraged her to strip everything, seeing the hunger in her tight nipples. She caused me to uncover, and afterward, I pulled her back into my arms, proceeding with my delicate stroking of her back.
I could feel the strain working in her body, so before she got excessively disappointed, I spun her around and pulled her back into me.

"God, yes!" she groaned as my chicken found the separation between the cheeks of her rear end. My hands rose to locate her stressing bosoms as she pushed her butt once again into me. Her head lolled back when I palmed her bosoms, shutting my fingers to pull and turn her nipples. I began somewhat delicate. However, I expanded the pressing factor to her whines of consent. Amy pushed her rear end profoundly into my chicken, and I changed her nipples hard.

"Eric, I'm ablaze! Pleasssse," she asked.

"We should get to your bed," I coordinated.

Amy snatched my hand and, in a real sense, hauled me to her bed. She grabbed the covers and tossed them back, imprudent of where they landed. As yet holding my hand, she opened her end table and pulled out a jug of lube, giving it back to me. She let go and afterward loosened up face down on the bed, spreading her legs somewhat and climbing her rear end out of sight. I paused for a minute to savor the sight: a delightful lady, horny too much, spread out before me, standing by eagerly for me to loot her tight ass.

"You are wonderful, Amy," I murmured.

"Get your hands on this wonderful body," she directed.

I burned through no time and moved alongside her. She can be wriggled underneath me, hungry for my touch. At long last, I offered it to her.

"Yessss," she murmured.

My fingers followed over the hurling skin of her rear end, so delicate yet so firm underneath. I helped remember our first night together when she urgently attempted to get my fingers on her indirect access. This time, she didn't need to stress. I let my fingers plunge over her private spot; at that point, I went to kneading the ring of muscle. A ceaseless series of murmurs and murmurs disclosed to me that I was doing the correct things.

When I felt her ring unwind, I went after the lube and flicked open the top. Amy's breath trapped in her throat, and her rear end climbed up eagerly.

I sprinkled some lube on a finger, at that point, but it at her rear end.

"Ummmmmm," she murmured, and I felt her delicately push out, loosening up her sphincter for me. My finger pushed inside, gradually, tenderly, getting access to her most private space. I halted at her subsequent ring and hung tight for it to unwind completely before I pushed in. At that point, I delicately pulled out and gradually pushed in further.

"Ohhhh, God," Amy moaned with her face immovably squeezed into the sleeping cushion. Her butt waved noticeable all around, pushing back when I pushed inside and pulling out when I did likewise. Before long, I had my finger covered to the root, and I gradually took long strokes in her can.

"Yeahhhhh," she empowered. As Amy got energized, she shifted her rear end further up and drove back more diligently, flagging me to push more earnestly myself. Before long, I was sawing my finger in profoundly, squeezing the remainder of my hand solidly against the cheeks of her can.

Amy whimpered and groaned, her hair spread around her covered face. All her consideration was on the finger doing sorcery to her can.

"Prepared for somewhat more?" I murmured.

"Pleasssse," she murmured back.

I gradually pulled out my finger and went along with it to another, sprinkling lube over them both. Amy's rear end bumped noticeable all around, missing the inclination inside her. She groaned when my fingers reconnected with her rear end.

I took this extremely lethargic, allowing Amy to acclimate to the sensation of size. Once more, she can lose, and I felt the opposition blur, and my fingers begin to spread the ring of muscle. They slid forward, at that point, held up at her subsequent ring. It loses, and I tenderly pushed inside. I let the ring open up; at that point, I slid my fingers out a piece, letting her rest. At that point back in, and this time she loses completely, willing me into her body. She pushed with her hips, and my fingers slid to the subsequent knuckle, joined by a robust groan. I halted there and gradually hauled somewhat way out.

"Ahhhhh," she energized on the following push. I went slightly further, at that point, back out. Each time, somewhat further. At last, I arrived at the end.

"So great," she mumbled. Her hips shifted up once more, and she offered me everything. Encouraged, I pushed more diligently and marginally turned with each stroke. Her back angled, and her can rose to meet me. She adored this.

We got into a musicality, and I sawed all the more solidly. I began turning my fingers in general, extending her open, preparing her if she needed to go further with this. I needn't have pondered.

"Eric, I need you inside me. Presently. I'm prepared," Amy coordinated.

"I realize you are," I replied. "I will lean against your headboard, and you will let yourself down on me."

"Awesome."

I slithered up next to her and settled back against the headboard, extending my legs before me. Amy lifted herself from the bed and rode my legs. I gave her the lube, and she sprinkled another measure over my rooster. I shuddered as her hand expertly jacked my chicken while she spread it around.

As yet holding my cockerel, Amy worked her knees forward until she lingered above me. I turned upward into her grin and the wild edges around her eyes. Amy deliberately situated my chicken at her back passage. We both murmured when the head settled at her external ring. Her eyes never left mine as she gradually brought down her hips. Shockingly, I didn't feel a lot of opposition as she opened to get me. I saw a similar inclination in her eyes. When I hit the internal ring, I felt opposition, yet Amy eased back down and let herself change. Unexpectedly, her eyes went wide as her internal ring loose. We both realized that this planned to work.

Amy's inward ring stroked the top of my chicken in hot velvet, sliding open gradually. She halted, rose marginally, and sunk. Her butt opened up somewhat more, and on the following plummet, the head slipped inside. My hands discovered her cheeks and stroked.

"Ohhhhhh," she relaxed. Her eyes grinned down at mine while she kept on working me inside her. I let her see the excitement she made in me. Her rear end was hot, smooth, and tight. Here and there she went.

"We're doing it," she pondered so anyone might hear.

"Definitely. Amy, you're inconceivable," I replied.

"This is so hot." Amy's hands came to the back and spread her cheeks separated. She angled her back and let herself down; I felt her cheeks brush my legs. Inside a couple of more strokes, she rested her full weight, my rooster drove right inside her.

I tore myself away from the staggering circumstance before me: a lovely, horny, hot lady straddling my hips with my rooster covered as far as possible in her rear end. I expected to concentrate elsewhere before my rooster emitted from the sheer sensuality; all things considered, Amy was a great spot to center, so I slid my hands around to her sticking bosoms, measuring and crushing the nipples.

"Yesssss," she murmured, sinking, so my cockerel skewered her rear end. I shifted my head back, and Amy tried to understand, dropping her lips down. She kissed me eagerly, driving her tongue into a sweet duel with mine.

Amy wound above me, her body reacting to the impeccable sentiments flowing all through. Her lips remained stuck to mine, and her breath came hot and hard.

I ensured I recollected which hand had avoided her can, and afterward, I let it trail down her side. I felt the grin all the rage.

"Gracious, no doubt," she groaned into my mouth. My hand gradually worked between her legs.

"Uhhhhhh." Her swollen pussy drove hard into my hand. It was doused with excitement, and I spread my fingers, keeping the pressing factor aberrant. Amy made it troublesome, contorting and driving her hips to drive her clit into me. I orbited around it, thinking hard to keep her baffled and hold me back from blowing my stack.

Amy sped her movements, enjoying long puffs all over my post. I could detect her workday from provisional movements to full-on stroking, secure in the joy transmitting from her butt. I yielded and let my fingers meet on her engorged clit.

"Ahhhh," she murmured in help. I twisted my pointer and let her groove her clit against it. She crushed her pussy into me, her breath coming in short wheezes. I kept on focusing on her clit, contemplating anything besides the goddess on the back of my hips.

"Goodness, God, Eric, I'm going to cum," she declared, pulling away from me.

I at long last permitted myself to think once more at her. Our association jumped to life, and I felt my shaft expand and solidify to unadulterated steel as I took a gander at the unalloyed desire emanating from Amy. I squeezed her clit in my fingers, and by the other hand, did likewise with her nipples, pulling hard. My climax worked down underneath, holding back to bubble over. I pressed back, holding off.

"Goodness, fuck, gracious fuck, gracious fuck," she gasped to her pushes. At that point, her body strained as her climax accumulated power. Her jeans got higher in pitch; at that point, she tossed her head back and shouted out as the principal fit tore through her. I felt her pussy tense; at that point, her breath got, and she shouted as her butt bounced back from my hard dick inside. I heard more indiscernible cries tear from her throat, and afterward, my climax requested its due. I wailed out my delivery as the primary impact flew up through my cockerel, showering profound into her shaking insides. Many shoots proceeded, the joy from her clasping ass almost terrible. My balls just kept on discharging into her.

After I don't have the foggiest idea how long, I felt her body droop against me. I delivered her nipples and diminished the tension on her clit while we both whimpered and jerked through the consequential convulsions. We took as much time as is needed.

At long last, I opened my eyes again to see hers looking profoundly into mine. I could detect the slight grin playing all over.

"Amazing. What occurred?" she pondered.

"That is called soul-smashing."

"Kid did it ever," she said and chuckled. I snickered with her, the two of us jerking with our most delicate spots associated. Amy quieted down and afterward twisted down to kiss me.

"Much obliged, Eric, for being so delicate with me. That was unfathomably acceptable."

"You are so welcome, Amy. I can't consider any place I'd preferably be."

We kissed profoundly, expressing gratitude toward one another with our lips.

"Prepared, Eric?" Amy pulled back and asked, looking again at me.

"Indeed, Amy," I reacted.

As yet associating with her eyes, I felt Amy raise herself from me. She jerked as my head passed her rings and afterward grinned at my whine when her sphincter shut over the withdrawing head. I slid down, and she brought down herself alongside me.

"Ahhhhh. I didn't understand how hardened I was," she conceded, gazing toward the roof.

"I think we were both somewhat enveloped with the occasion," I replied, coming down to delicately knead her thighs.

"Feels better," she relaxed.

I kept on working for my hands over her skin as her eyes shut. Feeling her floating off, I pulled the covers over us; at that point, I laid my head on her shoulder and hung my arm over her. She cuddled into me and moaned, and I permitted sleep to overwhelm me.

My psyche meandered in profound dreams, presumably energized by the ground-breaking lovemaking of the prior night. At last, the mist lifted, and morning's light separated through the window ornaments as I opened my eyes.

I just refreshed and delighted in the harmony, Amy's breathing without rushing next to me. At that point, it got, and she attracted a full breath as her eyes opened. They flickered and went to discover mine.

"Morning, Amy," I said tenderly, grinning at her.

"Morning, Eric." Amy grinned back and inclined in to kiss me. We embraced tight.
"What an evening," she said when she pulled back. "I rested awesome. You should?"

"Strong and profound," I replied. "I didn't wake until a couple of moments back. Everything is direct with the world."

"Allow me to figure. Incredible supper, extraordinary friend, awesome sex, profound rest. Is that your equation for bliss?"

"Basically," I snickered back. "You need to concede: It's difficult to beat."

"All things considered, the sex was incredible. You, at last, took me there, Eric."

"Furthermore, you were mind-boggling, Amy. It took all that I needed to hold back from blowing it the subsequent you brought down yourself onto me."

"I could see it in your eyes," she said, grinning. "In any case, at that point, the tables turned when I came. I've felt nothing that extraordinary."

"You were completely lost," I thought back. "Head tossed back; creature clamors coming from your throat. It was the most blazing thing I've at any point seen."

Amy reddened. "It's a touch of humiliating to concede the amount I preferred that."

I grinned back. "You were open and helpless. I cherished it."

"You're the one person I can open up with," she said.

"Never show signs of change," I replied.

Amy's arms lurked around me and pulled me in a warm embrace, saying everything with her body.

"Prepared for a shower?" Amy asked when we, in the end, unraveled.

"Good thought," I replied. We helped each other up and cushioned into the restroom connected at the hip.

Soaping her back, I posted an inquiry. "Amy, would you say you were OK with me contacting you after my fingers had been in your secondary passage?"

She giggled. "I don't think I even saw, yet indeed, I'm fine. Your hands felt very great on my chest, and I realize you care where you put them. Keep it up."

"Keep it up, huh? So there will be a subsequent time?"

"Goodness, no doubt. There is unquestionably going to be a subsequent time." I burst out chuckling, and Amy went along with me.

"How about we get completed, and I'll prepare you breakfast. I'm insatiable," I said.

"Need to get your solidarity back in the wake of bewitching me?"

"Precisely."

We wrapped up, and I discovered breakfast trimmings in Amy's fridge. "Anticipating organization?" I inquired.

"I calculated that I'd have some horny person over this end of the week and that he would require food following a night with me."

"You're not kidding," I concurred. I got occupied while she sat at a barstool.

"Sort of amusing to have another person cook in my home," she noticed.

"Simply recollect, few out of every odd horny person treats you this well."

"No person has at any point treated me that well, in bed or out."

"No young lady's always treated me that well possibly," I replied, turning upward from our omelets to see her moving eyes. "Off by a long shot."

"Not even Lisa?" she asked wickedly.

She found me napping, yet I immediately recuperated. "Lisa and I were a decent pair. However, there is something in particular about us, Amy, that goes past anything I've known."

"I know precisely what you mean," she chuckled. "Yet, I prefer to prod you."

"No doubt, I don't see that evolving."

"You wouldn't need it to." I turned upward, and she winked. I snickered, realizing she was correct.

We went bicycling, getting down to the stream, and having a nibble for a break. In transit home, we accelerated by a recreation center and enjoyed a reprieve under an overhanging tree. We both set down and turned upward into the leaves.

"Eric, thanks again for the previous evening. It was stunning. It didn't do any harm, and you felt great inside me."

"I'm a fortunate person to get expressed gratitude toward for what we did the previous evening," I explained a laugh from Amy. "In any case, my pleasure. At the point when two individuals set aside the effort to fabricate trust and involvement in butt-centric sex, it tends to be phenomenal. You've figured out how to confide in me, and all the more significantly, you've figured out how to confide in yourself. When I gave what you call my 'little discourse regarding the matter,' that is the thing that I implied. I'm truly happy that you delighted in it."

Amy grasped my hand and pressed hard.

We went through the end of the week generally together, visiting companions and having intercourse. I wondered again at how much fun Amy was to be around. I staggered out of her bed Monday morning and returned to my place to prepare for work.

"Jennifer might want to meet you for a beverage," Amy said sometime after that via telephone.

"Just me?" Like any person, I was playing this mindfully.

"Just you. I revealed to her I'd inquire. I think she has a few things she needs to advise you. Likely about me, or us. She's an old buddy, so I heed her gut feelings. Keen on hearing what she needs to say?"

"You're not worried she will share some profound, dim, mystery or qualm?"

"You've seen her glance at us, Eric. Does she appear as though she has any hesitations?"

"No, she sure doesn't," I conceded. "No doubt, I'd be glad to meet her. Perhaps I can acquire some influence over you, in any case."

"Try not to think you have enough as of now?"

"Never damages to have more, particularly with a sorceress like you."

Amy snickered. "No doubt about it."

So that is the way I wound up holding up Friday night at the place Jennifer proposed. Tasteful, with barely enough commotion to make private discussion conceivable. I didn't stand by well before she showed up, decked out in a sundress. Luckily, I had followed Amy's recommendation and dressed modestly.

"You look shocking, Jennifer," I said. "What would I be able to get you?"

"My, my, a commendation and a courteous offer. Amy's doing great with you. Gin and tonic, bless your heart." Jennifer sunk into the seat I offered, folding her legs and showing a ton of tanned thigh. Her brunette hair fell down her shoulders, outlining a rich face overwhelmed by puncturing green eyes. I painstakingly got my eyes far from her chest. However, I could detect that a trace of cleavage drove the eye down to pleasantly expanding bends. Jennifer grinned at all that entered my thoughts.

"Such a refined man," she murmured. "Feel somewhat shrewd, meeting another lady while your sweetheart is at home?"

"A bit, yes. So I'm glad that the lady's such acceptable organization."

Jennifer giggled. "Eric. You are simply the fiend! You're finishing this piece of the assessment incredibly well. Presently, how is your mom? I recall conversing with her when she visited."

I reacted, realizing that Jennifer was looking for her chance to jump. She took as much time as is needed, and we both visited pretty much all way of things.

"Like another?" I asked when her glass was vacant.

"If it's not too much trouble."

Our beverages came, and she got hers. I did likewise, and similarly, as I was going to taste, she hit me.

"Amy truly prefers you, you know."
I played it as cool as possible, taking a taste and reclining while I purchased time. I'd generally experienced difficulty reacting to that line, beginning back in 2nd grade.

"Presumably not however much I like her," I said, feeling satisfied with an answer that didn't sound weak or self-important.

She grinned. "I'm not entirely certain about that. Yet, I am certain that neither of you realizes how profound it goes. How should you? You have a lifetime to discover."

"A lifetime, huh?"

Jennifer didn't reply. She just took a gander at me.

"At any rate," she went on, "I needed to help you both out. You're both made for one another. Yet, in the long run, something Amy will get under your skin. When that occurs, you will recollect this discussion and the amount you value everything about Amy. What an incredible individual and companion she is. How athletic and excellent she is. How much fun she is. Also, in particular, how underhanded she is. She can be a guiltless young lady, an intelligent competing accomplice, and each man's wet dream—any way she picks. Do you hear what I'm saying?"

"I think you know the response to that, Jennifer."

"Advise me, Eric, so you'll recall. What is it about Amy that you enjoy most?"

"She simply quite loads of amusing to be near. She causes me to remain alert, positively."

"She's your equivalent, Eric. She's your sidekick, presently and until the end of time. There aren't numerous that can make that cut."

"A little commendation for me? I don't think I've at any point heard that from you, Jennifer. I'm complimented."
She grinned, a wide, certified grin from somewhere inside. "I generally give my #1 individuals the most hellfire. On the off chance that you'd attempted your karma with me, Eric, you may be shocked where it would have driven. In any case, I'm cheerful you didn't. Amy is the young lady for you, and you are certainly the kid for her. Ensure you love her. She's shining so brilliant at present; I'll realize when you're not treating her right."

I snickered. "You have a method of simply knowing things, Jennifer."

"What's more, even I fail to understand the situation, some of the time," she moped. Her green eyes fixed on mine. "I need to withdraw a specific assertion I made about what ladies need and don't need."

I felt my cheeks get hot. "I'll give you a pass on whatever it is that is no joke."

Jennifer laughed. "Amy, let me free similarly. It was amusing to make her wriggle—the odds don't come that regularly. You by the same token."

I grinned back at her.

"In some cases, quietly makes the most intelligent answer, does it not?" she said gently.

"In reality."

Jennifer burst out snickering. "This little meeting is significantly more fun than I suspected it would be."

"You have an intriguing origination of the word 'fun,' however at that point do as well, I."

"Thus does Amy," Jennifer added. "Presently, I wouldn't manage my work without separating, in any event, something more that you enjoy about her. Any thoughts?"

"Definitely," I said, investigating Jennifer's eyes. "Amy dives deep—way profound. There's a great deal to investigate, and I like investigating."

"Both your answers were about who Amy is within, and that has a backbone. Certainly, she's perfect. However, there are other dazzling young ladies. Me, for example."

I dunked my head in affirmation.

"However, there's nobody very like her, is there?"

"That is the thing that my heart advises me." Wow, I had said a ton.

Jennifer grinned. "Much obliged for sharing that, Eric. You let your gatekeeper down a piece; however, your heart needed to. I'll save that for an uncommon time with Amy. She'll cherish you even more for advising me."

I bowed my head again. At that point, I turned upward. "Much obliged to you, Jennifer."

Those green eyes fixed on me once more. "Say more."

"Meeting me; having this discussion. It shows you care about Amy—a great deal, and that you care about me. Likewise, I can feel something coming from Amy through you. You're shining all in all too, for your companion."

"Perceptive, Eric. My pleasure. Presently, I'd best be going soon, before this meeting turns out to be more enjoyable than it ought to. You'll recall what we discussed?"

I investigated her eyes. "Indeed. I will recollect."

"Amy said she'd recall too," she added, getting up. I got up with her. She inclined in and kissed me on the cheek. "Fortunate fiend," she murmured before turning around and strolling off. I realized she needed me to ponder who she implied. In any event, I got an opportunity to look at her as she danced out the entryway—she realized she looked great.

"Decent woman," the barkeep advertised.

"Very," I concurred.

I called Amy when I got to the vehicle. She didn't reply.

Afterward, she called.

"We both chuckled when your call came in. We had a wagered on what amount of time it would require."

"Indeed, even I'm savvy enough to assemble my young lady after conference one of her companions for a beverage."

Amy chuckled. "I'm taking you out this evening, Eric. Jennifer gave an exceptionally certain report on her little mission. Said that you were unbelievable—that you did everything right. She needed to stretch out the great parts—a lot to advise me in one day. You should have truly turned on the appeal."

"I'm adulating her if this doesn't work out."

Amy's snicker made me giggle also. "At any rate, Mr. Comic, get here."

Amy offered me an incredible supper, her radiance elevating the great vibes. Driving back, she investigated.

"Jennifer enlightened me concerning how she dressed to execute and how you enjoyed her yet kept your look cautiously on her eyes. She unquestionably saw that you needed to breeze through her little assessment. Might you want to go along with me for another little test this evening? This time, it's about the amount you can take a gander at all of my body."

"I like that test."

"I figured you would."

We spent another extraordinary end of the week together, including some incredible lovemaking. We kept in contact via telephone during the week, intending to meet Friday after work. Sleep time Thursday night, my telephone rang.

"Hi, Amy, what's going on with you?" I replied.

Her voice was low and guttural. "I need something truly downright awful; you're the solitary individual who can offer it to me."

My chicken mixed—this sounded intriguing. "Anything. How might I help?"

"Anything? I'll need to consider that. Yet, I understand what I need at this moment. I'm laying bare on my bed, face down. There are candles all over. I need something from you, seriously, profoundly. Would you be able to come over and help?"

My cockerel was rock hard. "I'll be directly finished."

"Leave your garments by the entryway. Rush."

I rushed, opening and facilitating her entryway open to see delicate candlelight. I stepped in, bolted the entryway behind me, and leaped out of my garments. A path of candles drove back to her room. I followed them to the glimmering light pouring from her open entryway.

"Amy..." my breath trapped in my throat.
"Eric. Much thanks to you such a great amount for coming." She was loosened up on the bed, candles all over, and a container of ointment close to her rear end. My heartbeat jumped in any event 30 pulsates.

"I'm so animated, so horny, so disappointed," she proceeded. "Do you understand what I need?"

I peered down to see her legs marginally spread, her knees drove into the bed, and her rear end pushing into the air. Her hands were under her chest, playing with her nipples.

"I think I have it sorted out," I laughed. "Furthermore, I can assist with your little issue." I loosened up on my side adjacent to her. "Might you want to cuddle once more into me and let me play with you for a piece?"

"Ohhhh, I'd love that," Amy answered, folding once again into me. Her can discovered my rooster, and she wriggled until I was settled safely between her cheeks. She pushed back hard, groaning and crushing. I stretched around to palm a bosom, testing its weight and feeling the hard stub of her nipples sticking out. I accumulated my fingers and pressed the nipples, hauling them out and curving.

"Yeesssss," she murmured, pushing her butt into my cockerel. I felt the slight harshness of her butt haul along the underside. Amy was ablaze, and I let her fabricate the warmth higher. She undulated into me for a few minutes, and her butt kept climbing until the top of my chicken discovered her secondary passage. She murmured and wound, attempting to get me inside her. My precum had slicked everything back there, and Amy stressed to utilize that as oil. I grinned to myself—she needed it terrible. She was exactly where I needed her.

"OK, angel. Back on your belly."

"Ummmmmm." She turned over and spread her legs, climbing her can up. I got the ointment and showered some over a finger, at that point, slid it down to prod her opening. She wriggled under me, battling to get my finger further in her rear end. At last, I kept my finger still to allow her to pierce herself. With a long groan, she lifted her butt, and my finger slid inside without any problem. Amy began shaking her hips, siphoning my finger to and fro. I could feel how loosened up she was as I began winding inside her. On one of her pushes, I pushed too.

"Oh," she murmured when I reached as far down as possible, the remainder of my hand possessively palming her butt. I let her enjoy the vibe of giving over her rear end for some time; at that point, I gradually pulled out to the sound of her whining.

I showered more lube on two fingers now and moved them back to her opening. All the more tenderly this time, I let her wriggle against them and gradually draw them inside. Her external ring-opened effectively; however, I stopped at her inward ring. Amy murmured, and I felt her unwind and push out. My fingers moved internally, and I stopped, retreated somewhat; at that point, let her draw them inside once more. In a couple of cycles, I was covered once more to another moan of fulfillment from Amy.

Once more, I let Amy push into me while I tenderly curved my fingers, loosening up the full circuit of her sphincter. I likewise fixed on Amy, learning about her fervor level and her availability for additional. She was turned on yet additionally profoundly loose, completely partaking in the thing we were doing together. I could discover no tension of what was to come. My eyes revealed to me a similar story. Amy's body squirmed under me; her fingers braced to her nipples.

"You prepared for me inside you?"

"I thought you'd never ask," she reacted from someplace far away. Before I could say much else, she drew her knees forward and lifted herself, climbing her rear end into the air with my fingers covered inside. I saw her draw her arms in and raise her chest too, laying on her elbows with her arms crossed under her, pulling at her hanging nipples. I didn't think it conceivable; however, my rooster solidified further at sight. I let her become acclimated to this new position; at that point, I flipped the top open on the lube and showered another segment onto my rooster with my other hand.

I rearranged forward and rested the top of my rooster adjacent to my fingers, sawing all through her.

"Eric. If it's not too much trouble."

I yielded and gradually pulled out my fingers to another delicate cry from Amy. I got the top of my chicken situated at her passageway and let her set the tone. She moaned and gradually propelled herself back. I felt the head open up her external sphincter; at that point, I felt the pressing factor from the internal ring. Amy stepped back somewhat, at that point pushed back once more. Her inward ring gradually extended, feeling like a delicate wave riding along the top of my chicken. It wasn't such a lot of infiltrating feeling as it was a feeling of her unwinding. Out of nowhere, the pressing factor facilitated.

"Gracious, God," she murmured. We both realized that I was in. Amy stopped to acclimate to the new sensations; at that point, she began shaking her hips gradually, drawing me more profound and afterward pulling back. Her passage was a heater, washing my cockerel in fluid warmth and pressing factor. I watched my rooster logically sink into her until her cheeks contacted my crotch.

"This feels so great," she relaxed.

"This feels fabulous," I replied. Indeed, she felt so fabulous that I drew my concentrate totally onto her, deferring the spring of gushing lava working inside me. I followed my fingers over her legs and back, feeling the sparkles stream between us. Amy crookedly contorted her hips, investigating and drawing out all the sensations inside and around her can. Her groans and whines authenticated the crude delight flowing through her body. I gradually pushed and pulled, letting her control the speed and profundity.

At that point, I saw it—the development of one of her hands back between her legs. She dropped her head down to consistent herself on the bed, and afterward, she moaned as her fingers discovered her elusive folds.

She began moderate, not having any desire to race to climax excessively fast. I could tell: she was mixing the new sensations from her rear end with the recognizable shiver of her pussy lips. I let her investigate.

Before adequately long, her body changed gear, and she moved from the conditional to the sure. He can be pushed back hard, and I met her pushes. She moaned, crushing her hips each time we reached as far down as possible. Her fingers got a move on her pussy, incidentally stimulating my balls. Amy was in the zone, ass brimming with rooster and cherishing it.

Is there anything better than this? A perfect lady turned on to excess, moving on the finish of my cockerel. Even better, she adored me, and if I was straightforward with myself, I cherished her comparably much.

Amy's breath presently came in snorts, coordinated with her shaking into me. We began to skip into one another, and I got her hips to pull her back with power.

"Goodness, screw yes," she moaned. Her fingers gave her pussy an exercise that I could feel in her rear end. Enough messing about. She was pushing for a climax—presently.

"That is it, child," I empowered. "Ride it hard." I crushed down on the ejection, taking steps to blow inside me, trusting I could make it until Amy was prepared.

"Gracious, better believe it. I'm going to cum soon," she gasped. Little pinpricks of work broke out on her skin. She pushed, and bent, and wheezed her way into unadulterated desire. I could feel her muscles tense, and afterward, I knew it: she was past the final turning point.

"I'm cumming!" she shouted and smashed into me. I met her and hung on. Her voice broke up into throaty snorts and groans as she came, hard. Her rear end beat around my bar and afterward bounced back, making her screech in enjoyment. Her climax tore my own from profound inside me, and I yelled as my semen battled and erupted past her grasping sphincter, multiplying the joy.

My memory of the following a few minutes is murky, involved as I was by thoughtless happiness. Nonetheless, I have a dream of Amy tossing her head back, gutting out a climax that was so ground-breaking it was practically difficult. She whimpered and groaned through the withdrawals, really imprudent of what she resembled.

We gradually returned to the real world, jerking with the delayed repercussions as usual. Amy measured her pussy, and I remained somewhere inside her, the two of us drawing out the last leftovers of our association.

"Gracious. My. God." Amy at last shouted.

"Soul-smashing?"

"For sure."

I grinned. "You were genuinely delightful."

Amy laughed. "So you think a young lady shouting out in thoughtless bliss is lovely, huh?"

"Without fail."

We ultimately got unraveled and set down close to one another for a rest.

"Like to share a shower before we rest?" Amy inquired.

"Showering with a lovely young lady? I'm generally up for that."

"Presumably. Presently go kick the water off, entertaining person."

I stood and offered a hand out to her. She grinned and took it, glancing brilliant in her post-orgasmic sparkle. She shooed me into the restroom to kick the water off. While I was changing the splash, I detected her coming in and putting something on the fenced-in shower area's highest point.

At the point when I ventured back to allow the water to warm, she pulled me to her for an embrace and kiss.

"Much obliged to you, Eric. That was fabulous."

"Amy, similar to what I said previously. I don't think you should express gratitude toward me."

She giggled. "Keep up the commendations, Eric. You'll get wherever with them."

She tried things out and pulled me inside. We began soaping each other up, and I could detect something energetic in her blue eyes. At the point when I got to her bosoms, she gasped and groaned.

"Get them truly spotless," she said a little energetically. My rooster blended. This young lady kept on astounding me.

Amy came up and kissed me. "Possibly, if I pivot, your hands will fit them better." With that, she spun around and settled back against me. I took my hands back to her bosoms, and she moved my chicken between the cheeks of her butt.

"No doubt. Ridiculously, clean," she coordinated. At the point when she shifted her head back for a kiss, my rooster solidified. She groaned into my mouth and began granulating her can maneuver into me.

She was hot and needing. Her nipples hardened in my grasp, and I took them in my fingers. Amy murmured her consent, and I began rolling the hard stubs. She can be moved around my chicken, and I accept her groans as clues to press and pull her nipples harder. Amy's tongue consumed in my mouth.

Amy broke our kiss to curve her back, and I felt the slight unpleasantness of her butt haul along the underside of my cockerel.

"I could do it once more—on the off chance that you need to," she said, glancing back at me.

"Is it accurate to say that you are certain?"

"Lube's up on the railing. That disclose to you how sure I am?" she said energetically. If her words didn't persuade me, I had her body crushing all over me for proof of her energy.

For an answer, I dropped my hands onto her can cheek and pulled them separated, crushing my rooster profound into her break.

"Gracious, God," she shouted, smashing her butt back against me. I got my hands back on her bosoms and pressed her nipples hard. Amy was in the mind-set to need it somewhat harsher.
"Yesssss," she murmured. I let her crush against me, topping her energy level.

After a spell, her butt moved, and I realized she was searching out the top of my cockerel. I dropped a hand to control it to her pucker, and she groaned. I reared up to the divider and inclined toward it, letting her direct the pressing factor she needed to apply.

Amy tried to understand, granulating back against me. She bent and squirmed her rear end, attempting to pull me inside with the abundant pre-cum spilling out of my cockerel. The head had just vanished into her inviting external ring. Alright, she truly needs it, I pondered internally. I came up to get the lube, not needing her enthusiasm to push things excessively quickly.

"Ummmmm," Amy murmured when she heard the snap of the container. I thought about releasing her straight with my rooster; however, I saved that for one more day. She may need a little agony later on, yet these first occasions should be loose and simple. I sprinkled some lube over a finger and began a similar delicate extending routine I did previously. Amy made it go quicker this time—she was hot to jog. When she was sawing effectively on two fingers, I got my chicken lubed and put it at her passage.

"Goodness, definitely," she inhaled, and she began pushing once more into me. With me inclining toward the divider, Amy was in finished control. She went much quicker than I would have, and soon my head could feel the velvet touch of her inward ring opening up. Amy kept consistent tension on me, and I slid past.

We panted together, lost in the sensations. Amy worked to and fro, driving me profound into her. At the point when her cheeks contacted my crotch, she moaned in triumph. On the two or three strokes, she had her cheeks straightened against me.

"God, this is acceptable," she shouted, delighting in the capacity to do anything she desired. I could feel increasingly more of her weight pin me back as she pushed further than I could at any point have done. I watched her hand sneak down between her legs, and I got my own hands back on her swollen nipples, coordinating the pressing factor she concerned me.

Amy began contorting her can with each stroke, getting bunches of skin contact before straightening against me. Her fingers worked her pussy with firm strokes that I could feel through my chicken.

Luckily, I had exhausted my balls into her once effectively tonight, so I had the option to unwind about blowing it too early. I reclined and enjoyed seeing Amy's body squirming in delight, her hair hanging in wet strands down her back. This was all her, and she was cherishing working my chicken profound into her guts.

Amy's fingers got a move on, and I felt them move to focus on her clit. I let my body react to hers, and she drew me along the street to the peak. My cockerel pistoned easily in the hot, tight touch of her back passage.

Her heaves expanded in pitch, and her fingers sped to a haze. My climax pooled in my balls, and the pressure transmitted out through my appendages. I peered down, and Amy's body was unbending, simply shaking on her feet to hammer into me.

"Gracious, God, I'm cumming once more!" she cried, and afterward, I felt the fits tear through her can. Amy lost it, shaking and snorting roughly through another unbelievable climax. Her peak dispatched my own, and I blew another heap profound into her entrails. I had barely sufficient synapses working on getting Amy to hold her back from falling over in the shower.

Much the same as in the past, we both whimpered and jerked our way back to earth.

"Amazing." I didn't have the foggiest idea of what else to say.

"Soul-smashing," she said and laughed. I jerked with my touchy rooster still in her can making her snicker stronger. We both wound up chuckling even though wheezes accentuated my snickers.

"Should I show leniency?" she inquired.

"If it's not too much trouble."

Amy tenderly pulled forward, and I gradually pulled out from her passage. Her sphincter shut over my head, and we both bounced a little as I pulled free. Amy extended back upstanding and turned around. I investigated her eyes and pulled her nearby for a kiss.

"You're unrealistic," I moaned when we pulled back.

Amy's blue eyes moved, and she stuck me to the divider for another long kiss.

In the end, we unraveled and got tidied up, this time with no further extracurricular exercises. We got each other dry, and I kept Amy's give over to the bed. We moved in and spooned together, expressing gratitude toward one another for the night and both falling profoundly sleeping.

The caution pulled us back from our sleep. We bounced in for another speedy shower.

"Last time we were in here, you exploited me," Amy said energetically.

"Uh, right," I replied. "I view at it more as assisting an urgent lady with getting what she painfully required."

"What's more, you did it so well. Possibly I'll require you to do that once more."

"I sure as damnation trust so."

Amy chuckled and smacked my can.

"Thus, advise me, Amy," I proceeded. "What might you have done if I was unable to come over?"

Amy gazed toward me, straight at me. "How about we see, Eric. I call you and offer a night with an ideal piece of ass. Some way or another, I had an inclination that you'd acknowledge. Yet, on the off chance that you hadn't been home, I surmise I would have quite recently fantasized about what might occur and deal with it myself. Understand what I mean?"

I chuckled. "I do. Also, you're correct. You have my number similar to your butt."

"Incidentally," she said, gazing toward me. "It was phenomenal. I'm happy I've done this little project as you would prefer. As you said, when

I'm that horny, I think just about the positive sentiments to come, and I'm completely loose about the thing we're doing."

"I'm happy you cooperated, Amy. You've been stunning."

"So are the climaxes. 'Soul-smashing' is correct. I can't accept how extreme they are."

"Your secondary passage needs to contract during your climax. However, my rooster forestalls that. You can then bounce back outward, extraordinarily expanding the delight. So now you get it."

"I 'got it' okay!" We both giggled and wrapped up, getting each other tidied up. After another seething kiss, I immediately halted my place to get some new garments and will work.

We went through one more end of the week together and wound up Sunday night at Amy's place. She made us supper, and we competed and giggled our way through another dinner.

I whirled the wine in my glass and investigated at Amy. "I believe it's an ideal opportunity to talk about something."

"Indeed?" she replied, her face a smidgen more genuine.

"However much I've delighted in it, I think we've satisfied a restricted meaning of our unique bundle bargain."

A touch of shading colored her cheeks. "I'll need to concur that you are right. However, you said 'slender.' What may a more extensive definition incorporate?"

I reclined. "A more extensive definition would be thorough in a literal sense. It could require some investment—quite a while—to satisfy. It's most likely something we'd need to consider before submitting ourselves."

Amy took a gander at me for quite a while. Her eyes shimmered. "I think you'll see me willing to examine the points of interest of a far-reaching bargain whenever you're prepared." She let that wait noticeably all around. "Meanwhile, I'm glad to expand the first arrangement with extra special care. It's been functioning admirably for me."

At last, we dedicated to an "extensive" arrangement, and I understood that a lifetime was too short to even think about understanding everything about Amy—goddess, mother, companion, sweetheart. She stayed "horny and baffled" all through, and I was glad to mitigate her strains and hold her indirect access fulfilled. She reddened a piece when the children got some information about how Mommy and Daddy met; however, we got by with the tale of us "living in a similar condominium unpredictable and running into one another constantly." Maybe sometime we'll tell the children somewhat a greater amount of reality.

Get up to 10 eBooks Totally FREE?!

If you are a devourer of erotic books and would like to receive up to 10 books immediately and totally **FREE** of charge, all you have to do is register for my list!
See below for more details!

Benefits of registration:

As a member of the list, you will receive the following benefits:

- 2 FREE books upon registration

- After registration, you have the possibility to get 8 additional books totally free of charge.
- The chance to have access in a totally free way - FOREVER AND AT ANY TIME - to ALL THE BOOKS already published and all of those that will be later on!
- The chance to participate in the creation of future books that I will publish!

I always listen to the ideas and requests of my readers and I strive to bring new and intriguing stories for all tastes.

You will have the opportunity to let me know not only what you think of my books, but also to suggest particular ideas such as the topics, settings, or characteristics of the main characters in the stories!

Every month, I will choose a proposal from the list of subscribers and make it into an erotic story.

If your idea is chosen, ONLY IF YOU WANT IT, you can be mentioned as a special thank you in the story!

Go to the link below and register now!

http://bit.ly/Scarlett_Collins